Re———
He———
breathe. It was close to mo———
had ended one session they'd been quick and
eager to start another. Where in the hell did all that
energy come from?

He knew she had to leave. So did he. But he didn't
want their one and only night together to end.
"You do know there is no reason why we can't—"

She quickly turned toward him and placed a finger
on his lips. "Yes, there is. I can't tell you my true
identity. It could hurt someone."

He frowned. As if reading his mind, she said,
"I don't have a husband. I don't even have a
boyfriend."

"Then who?" he asked. He probably had more
to lose than her since his campaign for Senate
officially began that day.

"I can't say. This has to be goodbye."

Dear Reader,

I am pleased to present to you Reginald Westmoreland's story. At long last!

Reggie was introduced in my very first Westmoreland book, *Delaney's Desert Sheikh,* as Delaney's partner in crime. By the end of the story, he had earned a special place in readers' hearts because he helped Delaney outsmart her overprotective brothers. Now, fifteen books later, it is time for his story to be told. I knew he would be the one to wrap up my books on the Atlanta-based Westmorelands.

I also knew he would be the one who would eventually become the Westmoreland to enter politics. And considering everything, doing so would not be an easy task. Especially if the woman your heart desires the most is the daughter of the man you're running against.

Neither Reggie nor Olivia Jeffries expect the explosive desire their initial meeting brings, and together they face many challenges. But they discover that no matter what, true love conquers all.

I've received a lot of letters and e-mails asking if Reggie's book is the end of the Westmorelands. My response is a resounding "No." There are more Westmorelands to come, and I look forward to introducing you to all the Denver-based Westmorelands. They are men you will continue to fall in love with.

Thank you for making the Westmorelands a very special family. I look forward to bringing you more books of searing desire and endless love and passion.

Happy reading!

Brenda Jackson

BRENDA JACKSON

TALL, DARK...
WESTMORELAND!

Silhouette®

Desire

Published by Silhouette Books
America's Publisher of Contemporary Romance

To the love of my life, Gerald Jackson, Sr., and to everyone
who has ever sent me a letter or e-mail to let me know how
much you've enjoyed the Westmorelands. This book is for you!

Withhold not good from them to whom it is due,
when it is in the power of thine hand to do it.
—*Proverbs* 3:27

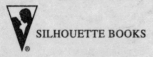 SILHOUETTE BOOKS

Recycling programs
for this product may
not exist in your area.

ISBN-13: 978-0-373-76928-5
ISBN-10:   0-373-76928-8

TALL, DARK...WESTMORELAND!

Books by Brenda Jackson

Silhouette Desire

*Delaney's Desert Sheikh #1473
*A Little Dare #1533
*Thorn's Challenge #1552
Scandal Between the Sheets #1573
*Stone Cold Surrender #1601
*Riding the Storm #1625
*Jared's Counterfeit Fiancée #1654
Strictly Confidential Attraction #1677
*The Chase Is On #1690
Taking Care of Business #1705
*The Durango Affair #1727
*Ian's Ultimate Gamble #1756
*Seduction, Westmoreland Style #1778
Stranded with the Tempting
   Stranger #1825
*Spencer's Forbidden Passion #1838
*Taming Clint Westmoreland #1850
*Cole's Red-Hot Pursuit #1874
*Quade's Babies #1911
*Tall, Dark...Westmoreland! #1928

*The Westmorelands

Kimani Romance

Solid Soul #1
Night Heat #9
Risky Pleasures #37
In Bed with the Boss #53
Irresistible Forces #89
Just Deserts #97
The Object of His
   Protection #113

Kimani Arabesque

Tonight and Forever
A Valentine's Kiss
Whispered Promises
Eternally Yours
One Special Moment
Fire and Desire
Something to Celebrate
Secret Love
True Love
Surrender

BRENDA JACKSON

is a die "heart" romantic who married her childhood sweetheart and still proudly wears the "going steady" ring he gave her when she was fifteen years old. Because she's always believed in the power of love, Brenda's stories all have happy endings. In her real-life love story, Brenda and her husband of thirty-six years live in Jacksonville, Florida, and have two sons.

A *New York Times* bestselling author of more than fifty romance titles, Brenda is a recent retiree who worked thirty-seven years in management at a major insurance company. She divides her time between family, writing and traveling with Gerald. You may write Brenda at P.O. Box 28267, Jacksonville, Florida 32226, by e-mail at WriterBJackson@aol.com or visit her Web site at www.brendajackson.net.

THE WESTMORELAND FAMILY

Scott and Delane Westmoreland

| John (Evelyn) | | | | | | | James (Sarah) | | | Corey (Abbie) |

Children of John (Evelyn):

②	③	④	⑤	⑦	①
Dare (Shelly) AJ, Allison	Thorn (Tara) Trace	Stone (Madison) Rock	Storm (Jayla) Shanna, Johanna	Chase (Jessica)	Delaney (Jamal) Ari, Arielle
⑥	⑪	⑧	⑨	⑭	⑮

Jared (Dana)	Spencer (Chardonnay) Russell	Durango (Savannah) Sarah	Ian (Brooke) Pierce, Price	Quade (Cheyenne) Venus, Athena, Troy	Reggie
⑫	⑬		⑩		

Clint (Alyssa) Cain	Cole (Patrina) Emilie, Emery	Casey (McKinnon) Corey

① Delaney's Desert Sheikh
② A Little Dare
③ Thorn's Challenge
④ Stone Cold Surrender
⑤ Riding the Storm
⑥ Jared's Counterfeit Fiancée
⑦ The Chase Is On
⑧ The Durango Affair
⑨ Ian's Ultimate Gamble
⑩ Seduction, Westmoreland Style
⑪ Spencer's Forbidden Passion
⑫ Taming Clint Westmoreland
⑬ Cole's Red-Hot Pursuit
⑭ Quade's Babies
⑮ Tall, Dark...Westmoreland!

One

There has to be another way for a woman to have fun, Olivia Jeffries thought as she glanced around at everyone attending the Firemen's Masquerade Ball, an annual charity event held in downtown Atlanta. Already she was gearing up for a boring evening.

It wouldn't have been so bad if she hadn't arrived from Paris just yesterday, after being summoned home by her father. That meant she had to drop everything, including plans to drive through the countryside of the Seine Valley to complete the painting she had started months ago.

Returning to Atlanta had required her to take a leave of absence from her job as an art curator at the Louvre. But when Orin Jeffries called, she hadn't hesitated to drop everything. After all, he was only the greatest dad in the entire world.

He had wanted her home after making the decision to run for public office, saying it was important that she was there not only for his first fund-raiser but also for the duration of his campaign. There would be a number of functions he would need to attend, and he preferred not to go with any particular woman on a regular basis. He didn't want any of his female friends to get the wrong idea.

Olivia could only shake her head and smile. Her divorced father had taken himself off the marriage block years ago. In fact, she doubted he'd ever allowed himself to be there in the first place. He dated on occasion, but he'd never gotten serious about any woman, which was a pity. At fifty-six, Orin Jeffries was without a doubt a very good-looking man. His ex-wife, who was Olivia's mom in genes only, had left a bad taste in Orin's mouth. A taste that the past twenty-four years hadn't erased.

Her two older brothers, Duan, who was thirty-six, and Terrence, who was thirty-four, had taken after her father in their good looks. And as in the case of their father, the thought of marriage was the last thing on their minds. In a way, she followed in her dad's footsteps as well. Finding a husband was the last thing on hers.

So there you had it. They were the swinging single Jeffries, although for the moment, nothing was swinging for her, Olivia thought. There were a few people at this ball who seemed to be having fun, but most, like her, were looking at their watches and wondering when proper etiquette dictated it would be okay to leave.

Whoever had come up with the idea of everyone wearing masks had really been off their rocker. It made her feel like she was part of the Lone Ranger's posse. And because all the money raised tonight was for the new wing at the children's hospital, in addition to the mask, everyone was required to wear a name badge on which was printed the name of a nursery rhyme character, a color of a crayon or a well-known cartoon or comic-book character. How creative.

At least the food was good. The first words out of her father's mouth when he'd seen her at the airport the day before had been, "You look too thin." She figured the least she could do was mosey on over to the buffet table and get herself something to eat. Hopefully, in a little while she could split.

Reginald Westmoreland watched the woman as she crossed the room, making her way over to the buffet table. He had been watching her for over twenty minutes now, racking his brain as to who she was. Mask or no mask, he recognized most of the women at the ball tonight. He knew almost every one of them because for years he had been immersed in the science of "lip-tology." In other words, the first thing he noticed about a woman was her lips.

He could recognize a woman by her lips alone, without even looking at any other facial feature. Most people wouldn't agree, but no two pairs of lips were the same. His brothers and cousins had denounced his claim and had quickly put him to the test. He had just as quickly proven them wrong. Whether you considered it a blessing or a curse, the bottom line was that he had the gift.

And there were other things besides her lips that caught his attention, like her height. She had to be almost six feet tall. And then he was struck by the way she fit into her elegantly designed black and silver beaded dress, the way the material clung to her shapely curves. He had noticed several men approach her, but she had yet to dance with any of them. In fact, it seemed that she was brushing them off. Reginald smelled a challenge.

"So, how is the campaign going, Reggie?"

Reginald, known to all his family as Reggie, turned to look at his older brother, divorce attorney extraordinaire, Jared Westmoreland. Just last week Jared had made the national news owing to a high-profile settlement he'd won in favor of a well-known Hollywood actor.

"It officially kicks off Monday. But now that Jeffries has decided to throw his hat into the ring, things should be rather interesting," he said, referring to the older man who would be his opponent. "With Brent, I have a good campaign manager, but I still feel it might be a tight race. Jeffries is well-known and well-liked."

"Well, if you need any help, let me know, although I'm not sure how much time I can spare now that Dana's expecting and all."

Reggie rolled his eyes. Just last month Jared had found out he was going to be a father. "Dana is going to be carrying the baby, Jared, not you."

"I know, but I'm the one who's been getting sick in the morning, and now I'm getting cravings. I never liked pickles until now."

Reggie couldn't help but smile over his wineglass. "Sounds like a personal problem to me." At the moment, his attention strayed from whatever Jared was saying. Instead, his gaze focused on the other side of the room. He noticed the woman whom he'd been watching sit down at a table. He had yet to see a man by her side, which meant she had come to the party alone.

"Umm, I wonder who she is?" he asked.

Jared followed Reggie's gaze and chuckled. "What's wrong? Don't you recognize the lips?"

Reggie shifted his gaze from the woman to his brother and frowned. "No, she's someone new. I definitely haven't met her before. Her lips don't give her away."

"Then I guess the only thing left for you to do is go over there and introduce yourself."

Reggie grinned. "I know they don't call you the sharpest attorney in Atlanta for nothing."

"Don't you know sitting alone at a party isn't good for you?"

Olivia swung her head around at the sound of the deep, throaty masculine voice to find a tall, handsome man standing beside her. Like everyone else, he was wearing a mask, but even with it covering half of his face, she knew he had to be extremely good-looking. In the dim lighting, her artist eye was able to capture all his striking features that were exposed.

First of all, there was his skin, flawlessly smooth and a shade of color that reminded her of rich, dark maple syrup. Then there was the angular plane of a jaw that supported a pair of sexy lips. The same ones that bestowed a slow smile on her. Apparently, he realized she was checking him out.

"In that case, I guess you need to join me," she replied, trying to remember the last time she'd been so outrageously forward with a guy and quickly deciding never. But the way the evening was going, she would have to stir up her own excitement. And now was as good a time as any to start. Maybe it was the fact that the party was so unrelentingly boring that made her long for a taste of the wild and reckless. The other men who had approached her hadn't even piqued her curiosity. She had no desire to get to know them better. But this man was different.

"I don't mind if I do," he said, easily sliding into the chair beside her while his eyes remained locked with hers. Her nose immediately picked up the scent of his cologne. Expensive. She quickly checked out his left hand. Ringless. Her gaze automatically went back to his face. Beautiful. Now he was smiling in earnest and showing beautiful white teeth.

"You're amused," she said, taking a sip of her punch but wishing she had something a little stronger.

Whoever he was, he was certainly someone worth getting to know, even if she was returning to Paris in a few months. That made it all the more plausible. It had taken her two years to get on full-time at the Louvre, and the hard work was just beginning. Once she returned, she would be working long hours, with little time to get her painting done. That was why she had brought her paints to Atlanta with her. She was determined to capture something worthwhile on canvas while she was here. The man sitting beside her would be the perfect subject.

"Flattered more than amused," he said, his voice reaching out and actually touching her, although she barely registered his words in her mind, because she was too busy watching the way his mouth moved. Sensuously slow.

She couldn't help wondering who he was. She had been gone from Atlanta a long time. After high school she had attended Pratt Institute in New York before doing her graduate work at the Art Institute of Boston. From there she had made the move to Paris, after landing a job as a tour professional, a glorified name for a tour guide.

He had to be around her brother Terrence's age, or maybe a year or so younger. She wondered if he would give her his real name, or if he would stick to the rules and play this silly little game the coordinators of the ball had come up with. His name badge said Jack Sprat. No wonder he was in such fine shape, she thought. Even in the tuxedo he was wearing, she saw broad, muscular shoulders and a nice solid chest. All muscles. Definitely no fat.

"So, Jack," she said, smiling at him the same way he was smiling at her. "What is such a nice guy like you doing at a boring party like this?"

He chuckled, and the sound sent goose bumps over her body. "Waiting to meet you so we can start having some fun." He glanced at her name badge. "Wonder Woman."

The smile that touched the corners of her mouth

widened. She liked him already. "Well, trust me when I say, it's a *wonder* that I'm here at all. I really want to be someplace else, but I promised the person who paid for this ticket that I'd come in his place. And since it's all for charity, and for such a good cause, I decided to at least make an appearance."

"I'm glad you did."

And Reggie meant it. He'd thought she had a beautiful pair of lips from afar, but now he had a chance to really study them up close. They were a pair he would never forget. They were full, shapely, and had luscious-looking dips at the corners. She had them covered in light lip gloss, which was perfect; any color would detract from their modish structure.

"We've exchanged names, and I'm glad to make your acquaintance, Jack," she said, presenting her hand to him.

He grinned. "Likewise, Wonder."

The moment their hands touched, he felt it and knew that she did, too. Her fingers quivered on his, and for some reason, he could not release her hand. That realization unnerved him. No woman had ever had this kind of effect on him before, not in all his thirty-two years.

"Are you from Atlanta?"

Her voice, soft and filled with Southern charm, reclaimed his attention.

"Yes, born and raised right here," he said, reluctantly releasing her hand. "What about you?"

"Same here," she said, looking at him as if she could see through his mask. "Why haven't we met before?"

He smiled. "How do you know that we haven't?"

Her chuckle came easily. "Trust me. I would remember if we had. You're the type of man a woman couldn't easily forget."

"Hey, that's my line. You stole it," he said jokingly.

"I'll give it back to you if you take me away from here."

He didn't say anything for a minute but just sat there studying her face. And then he asked, "Are you sure you want to go off with me?"

She managed another smile. "Are you sure you want to take me?" she challenged.

Reggie couldn't help but laugh loudly, so loudly, in fact, that when he glanced across the room, his brother Jared caught his gaze and gave him a raised brow. He had five brothers in all. He and Jared were the only ones still living in Atlanta. He also had a bunch of cousins in the city. It seemed Westmorelands were everywhere, but he and Jared were the only ones who were here tonight. The rest had other engagements or were off traveling someplace.

A part of Reggie was grateful for that. He was the youngest of the Atlanta-based Westmorelands, and his brothers and cousins still liked to consider him the baby of the family, although he stood six-seven and was the tallest of the clan.

"Yes, I would take you in a heartbeat, sweetheart. I would take you anywhere you wanted to go."

And he meant it.

She nodded politely, but he knew she was thinking, trying to figure out a way she could go off with him and not take any careless risks with her safety. A woman couldn't be too trusting these days, and he understood that.

"I have an idea," he said finally, when she hadn't responded and several moments had passed.

"What?"

He reached into his jacket pocket and pulled out his cell phone. "Text someone you know and trust, and tell them to save my number. Tell them you will call them in the morning. When you call, they can erase the number."

Olivia thought about what he'd suggested and then wondered whom she could call. Any girl-friends she'd had while living here years ago were no longer around. Of course, she couldn't text her father, so she thought about her brothers. Duan was presently out of the city, since his job as a private investigator took him all over the country, and Terrence was living in the Florida Keys. She and her brothers were close, but it was Terrence who usually let her get away with things. Duan enjoyed playing the role of older brother. He would ask questions. Terrence would ask questions, too, but he was more easygoing.

Perhaps it was Duan's inquisitive mind that made him such a stickler for the rules. It had to be all those years he'd worked first as a patrolman and then as a detective for Atlanta's police department. Terrence, a former pro football player for the Miami Dolphins, knew how to have fun. He was actually the real swinging single Jeffries. He owned a nice club in the Florida Keys that really embodied the term *nightlife*.

Her safest bet would be to go with Terrence.

"Okay," she said, taking the phone. She sent Terrence a quick text message, asking that he delete the phone number from which the message was sent after hearing from her in the morning. She handed the phone back to him.

"Feel better about this?" he asked her.

She met his gaze. "Yes."

"Good. Is there any particular place you want to go?"

The safest location would be her place, Olivia thought, but she knew she couldn't do that. Her father was home, going over a campaign speech he would be giving at a luncheon on Monday. "No, but I haven't been out to Stone Mountain in a while."

He smiled. "Then Stone Mountain it is."

"And we'll need to go in separate cars," she said quickly. She had begun to feel nervous because she had never done anything like this in her life. What was she thinking? She got a quick answer when she met his gaze again. She was thinking how it would probably feel to be in this man's arms, to rub her hand across that strong, angular jaw, to taste those kissable lips and to breathe in more of his masculine scent.

"That's fine," he said in a husky voice. "You lead and I'll follow."

"And we keep on our masks and use these names," she said, pointing to her name badge.

He studied her intently for a moment before nodding his head. "All right."

She let out a silent breath. Her father was well-known in the city, and with the election just a couple of months away, she didn't want to do anything to jeopardize his chances of winning. Anything like having her name smeared in the paper in some scandal. Scandals were hard to live down, and she didn't want do anything that would be a nice addition to the *Atlanta Journal-Constitution*'s gossip column.

"Okay, let's go," she said, rising to her feet. She hoped she wasn't making a mistake, but when he accidentally brushed up against her when they headed for the exit, she had a feeling anything that happened between them tonight could only be right.

Reggie, as a rule, didn't do one-night stands. However, he would definitely make tonight and this woman an exception. The car he was following close behind was a rental, so that didn't give him any clues as to her identity. All he did know was that she was someone who wanted to enjoy tonight, and he was going to make sure she wasn't disappointed.

She'd indicated that she wanted to go someplace in Stone Mountain, and she was heading in that direction. He wondered if they would go directly to a place where they could be alone, or if they would work up to that over a few drinks in a club. If she wanted a night on the town first, there were a number of nightclubs to choose from, but that would mean removing their masks, and he had a feeling she intended for these to stay in place. Why? Was she as well-known around the city as he was? At least after Monday he would be. Brent Fairgate, his campaign manager and the main person who had talked him into running for the Senate, had arranged for campaign posters with his picture to be plastered on just about every free space in Atlanta.

Returning his attention to the car in front of him, he braked when they came to a traffic light. Just then his cell phone rang. He worked it out of his pocket. "Hello?"

"Where are you?"

He gave a short laugh. "Don't worry about me, Jared. However, I do apologize for not letting you know I was leaving."

"That woman you were with earlier isn't here, either. Is that a coincidence?"

Reggie shook his head, grinning. "I don't know. You tell me."

There was a pause on the other end. "You sure about what you're doing, Reggie?"

"Positive. And no lectures please."

"Whatever," came his brother's gruff reply. And then the call was disconnected.

The traffic began moving again, and Reggie couldn't help but think about how his life would change once the campaigning began. There would be speeches to deliver, interviews to do, television appearances to make, babies to kiss and so on and so forth. He would be the first Westmoreland to enter politics, and for him, the decision hadn't been an easy one to make. But Atlanta was growing by leaps and bounds, and he wanted to give back to the city that had given him so much.

Unlike his brothers, who had left town to attend college, he had remained here and had gone to Morehouse. And he had never regretted doing so. He smiled, thinking that the good old days were when he got out of college and, a few years later, when he opened his own accounting firm. At the time, his best buddy had been his cousin Delaney. They were only a few months apart in age and had always been close. In fact, he was the one who had helped Delaney outsmart her five overprotective brothers right after she finished med school and needed to get some private time. He had let her use his cabin in the mountains for a little rest and relaxation, without telling Dare, Thorn, Stone, Chase or Storm where she was. Lucky for him, his cousins hadn't broken his bones, as they had threatened to do, when they discovered his involvement. The good thing was that Delaney had met her desert sheikh and fallen in love at his cabin.

Reggie's attention was pulled back to the car in front of him when Wonder Woman put on her blinker to turn into the parking lot of the luxurious Saxon Hotel. He smiled. He liked her taste, but given that they were wearing masks, he wondered how this would work. And then he got an idea and immediately pulled his cell phone out of his jacket pocket to punch in a few numbers.

"Hello?"

Reggie could hear babies crying in the background. "This is Reggie. What are you doing to my nieces and nephew?"

He heard his brother Quade's laugh. "It's bath time, and nobody wants to play in the water tonight. What's up? And I understand congratulations are in order. Mom told me you've decided to run for the Senate. Good luck."

"Thanks." And then, without missing a beat, he said, "I need a favor, Quade."

"What kind of favor?"

"I need a private room at the Saxon Hotel here in Atlanta tonight, and I know Dominic Saxon is your brother-in-law."

"So?"

"So make it happen for me tonight, as soon as possible. And I need things kept discreet and billed to me."

There was a pause on the other end. "You sure about this, Reggie?"

He shook his head. It was the same question Jared had asked him moments ago. "Yes, Quade, I'm sure. And I don't expect any lectures from you, considering when and how my nieces and nephew were conceived."

"Go to hell, Reggie."

He smiled. "Not in front of the babies, Quade. And as far as going to hell, I'll go, but only after I get a night of heaven. So make it happen for me, Quade. I'll owe you. I'll even volunteer to fly in one day and babysit."

"Damn, she must be some woman."

Reggie thought about those lips he wanted so desperately to taste. "She is."

"I'll see what I can do." And then the call was disconnected.

Smiling and feeling pretty certain that Quade would come through for him, he watched as Wonder Woman parked her car, and then eased his car into the parking spot next to hers. As soon as she turned off the engine, he got out of his car and glanced around, making sure there weren't a lot of people about. She had parked in an area that was pretty empty, and he was grateful for that.

When he got to her side of the car, she rolled down the window and looked a little flushed. "Sorry. I guess I didn't think this far ahead."

He bent down and leaned forward against her door and propped his arms on the car's window frame and smiled at her. She smelled good, and she looked good. His gaze shifted from her eyes to her lips and then back to her eyes again. He couldn't wait to taste her lips.

"Don't worry. Tonight will end the way we want," he said, with certainty in his voice and all the while thinking that if Quade didn't come through for him tonight, he was liable to kill him. At her confused expression, he said, "I've made a call, and it will only be a few moments. I'll get a call back when things get set up."

Olivia eyed the man staring at her and tried to ignore the stirring in the pit of her stomach. She couldn't help wondering just who was he and what kind of connections he had. They had to be big ones if he was able to get them a room at the Saxon from the parking lot. Would they have to do the normal check-in?

One part of her brain was screaming at her, telling her that what she was contemplating doing was downright foolish and irresponsible. No good girl, certainly not one who'd been raised to be a proper young lady, would think about having a one-night stand with a stranger.

But then the other part of her brain, the one that was daring, as well as wild and reckless, urged her on. Go ahead, Libby. Have some fun. Live a little. You haven't been seriously involved with a man for almost two years. You've been too busy. You deserve some fun. What will it hurt as long as you've taken every precaution to make sure you're safe?

And at the moment she was safe. Terrence had this man's phone number, and the hotel was definitely a respectable one. And it was one she had selected, not him. But she had to admit, she felt a little silly with the two of them still wearing their masks. At least she had taken off her name badge.

"So, Wonder Woman, what's your favorite color?"

She couldn't help but smile. He evidently felt the tension and was making an attempt to ease it. "Lavender. What's yours?"

"Flesh tone."

She grinned. "Flesh tone isn't a color."

"Depends on who's wearing it," he said softly, and then his eyes flickered to her lips. She felt the intensity of his gaze just as if it was a soft caress. Suddenly, she felt the need to moisten her lips with her tongue.

"I wish you hadn't done that," he whispered huskily, leaning his body forward to the point where more of his face was in the window, just inches from her face.

A breathless sigh escaped from her lips. "What?" she asked in a strained voice.

"Tasted your own lips. That's what I want to do. What I'm dying to do."

"What's stopping you?"

Reggie thought that was a dare if ever he'd heard one. Deciding to take her up on it, he leaned his body in closer. She was tilting her head toward his face when suddenly his cell phone rang.

Damn. He reluctantly pulled back and pulled the cell phone from his jacket.

Olivia took that time to take a deep breath, and then she listened to his phone conversation.

"Yes?" he said into the phone.

She watched a huge smile brighten his face, and at the same time, she felt intense heat gather at the junction of her thighs.

"Thanks, man. I owe you one," he said. She then watched as he clicked off the phone and put it in his pocket. He glanced over at her. "Okay, Wonder Woman. Everything is set. We're on the sixteenth floor. Room sixteen thirty-two. Ready?"

She exhaled slowly. A part of her wanted to tell him that, no, she wasn't ready. She wanted to know how he'd arranged everything from a parking lot.

Another part of her needed to know how he was capable of making her feel things that no other man had ever made her feel before. How was he able to get her to take risks when she was the least impulsive person that had ever lived? At least she had been risk averse until she'd seen him at the party tonight.

She met his gaze, knowing this would be it. Once she got out of the car and walked into that hotel with him, their night together would begin. Was that what she really wanted? He was staring at her, and his gaze seemed to be asking her that same question.

She drew in a deep breath and nodded her head and said, "Yes, I'm ready."

He then opened the car door for her. "You go on ahead, and I'll follow within five minutes. The bank of elevators you should use is the one to the right of the check-in desk," he said.

"Okay."

He watched as she placed the strap of her purse on her shoulder before walking away. He smiled as she gracefully crossed the parking lot and headed toward the entrance to the hotel. He couldn't help but admire the way she looked in her dress, a silky number that swished around her legs whenever she made a movement. And she had the legs for it. Long, shapely legs that he could imagine wrapped around him, holding him inside her body during the heat of passion.

He was so into his thoughts that when she suddenly stopped walking, his heart nearly stopped beating. Had she changed her mind? Moments later he gave a deep sigh of relief when he realized she had stopped to remove her mask. He wondered if she would take the risk and turn around to let him see her face, voluntarily revealing her identity. He got his answer when she began walking again without looking back. He had a feeling that that was how the entire night would go. Identities and names would not be shared. Only passion.

He would respect her wishes, and when he joined her in the hotel room, his mask, too, would be back in place.

There was no doubt in his mind that this would be a night he would always remember.

Two

Olivia was grateful that no one seemed to pay her any attention when she walked into the huge lobby of the Saxon. It had always been her dream to spend a night in what had to be one of the most elegant hotels ever built. It was more stylish and extravagant than she had expected. There were only a few Saxons scattered about the country, in the major cities, and all had a reputation of providing top-quality service.

When she stepped onto the elevator that would carry her to the sixteenth floor, she couldn't help but again wonder about the man behind the mask and the connections he seemed to have. Reservations were hard to get because the hotel was booked far in advance, even as much as a year.

As she stepped out of the elevator and walked down the spacious hall, she studied the decor. Everything had a touch of elegance and class. With an artist's eye, she absorbed every fine detail of not only the rich and luxurious-looking carpet on the floor but also of the beautiful framed portraits that lined the walls. She would bet a month of her salary at the Louvre that those were original Audubon prints. If they devoted this much time and attention to the hallways, she could only imagine what one of the rooms would look like.

She wondered what Jack Sprat thought of her taste, since she was the one who'd guided him here. Of course, she would pay tonight's bill, since coming here was her idea. Connections or no connections, this place was her choice and not his, so it would only be fair. The last thing she wanted to do was come off as a thoughtless, high-maintenance woman.

Moments later she stood in front of room 1632. She didn't have a key and could only assume the door was unlocked. There was only one way to find out. She turned the handle and smiled when it gave way without a problem. She slowly opened the door and stepped into the room. Quickly closing the door, she glanced around, her eyes widening. This had to be a penthouse suite. She hadn't expected this, wasn't even sure she would be able to pay for it. She had figured on a regular room, which, though costly, would have been within her budget.

She was paid well, and loved Paris, but eventually she intended to return to the United States. She planned to open an art gallery in a few years, and that took money. Every penny she earned went into her special savings. Her father and brothers had promised to invest in the venture, but she felt that it was her responsibility to come up with the majority of the capital for her gallery. This little tryst was going to cost her. She would have to dip into her savings to pay for this suite. She wondered if just one night with a stranger could possibly be worth the sacrifice.

She crossed the room, drawn to the stately furnishings. She had stayed in nice hotels before, but there was something about a Saxon that took your breath away. Besides the elegant luxury that surrounded you, there was also the personalized service, culinary excellence and other amenities, which she had often heard about, but had yet to experience.

She walked through the sitting area to the bedroom. Her gaze moved from the plush love seat in the room to the bed. The bed was humongous and stately; the covering was soft to the touch. It felt as if you could actually lose yourself under it. The bedcoverings and curtains were done in an elegant red and a single red rose had been placed in the middle of the bed. Very romantic.

The connecting bath was just as stunning, with a huge Jacuzzi tub that sat in the middle of the floor, surrounded by a wall-to-wall vanity the likes of which she'd never seen in a hotel. Everything was his and hers, and the bathroom was roomy, spacious.

Nervously, she walked out of the bathroom and back into the bedroom and sat down on the edge of the bed.

When she was growing up, people had often said she was spoiled and pampered, and in a way, she had been. Being the only girl in the house had had its advantages. She had been only three years old when her mother left her father, ran off with a married man and destroyed not one, but two families. She would always admire her father for doing what had to be done to hold their family together. He'd worked long and hard hours as a corporate attorney and still had been there for her piano recitals and art shows and her brothers' Little League games. And one year he had even gotten elected president of the PTA. It hadn't been easy, and everyone had had to pitch in and help. And she could now admit that her brothers had made it easier for her.

Leaving home for college had been good for her. Against her father's and brothers' wishes, she had worked her way through college, refusing the money they would send her. She'd needed to encounter the real world and sink or swim on her own while doing so.

She'd learned how to swim.

She glanced at her watch. Chances were that Jack Sprat was on his way up, so now was not the time to get nervous. She had come on to him at the party, and he had come on to her. They were here because a night together was what they both wanted. So why was she thinking about hightailing it all of a sudden? Why were butterflies flying around her stomach? And what was with the darn goose bumps covering her arms?

She stood and began pacing. He would be here at any moment, so she stopped and took the time to put her mask back on. In a way she felt silly, but at the same time mysterious.

Olivia glanced at her watch again. She felt her body heating up just thinking about what would happen when he did arrive. To say she was fascinated by a complete stranger would be an understatement. If anyone had told her that within less than forty-eight hours of returning to Atlanta, she, Olivia Jeffries, would be involved in an affair to nowhere, she would not have believed them. Usually she was very conservative, but not tonight.

She caught her breath when she thought she heard footsteps coming down the hall. An anticipatory shiver ran down her spine, and she knew that in just a minute he would be there.

Reggie walked down the hallway, deep in thought. Some people engaged in casual affairs to pass the time or to feel needed. He was not one of them, and for some reason, he knew that the woman waiting on him in the hotel room wasn't, either. He would admit that there had been a few one-night stands in his history, back in the day at Morehouse, when he hadn't had a care in the world other than studying, making the grade and getting an easy lay. But now as a professional who owned a very prestigious accounting firm and as a political candidate, he picked his bed partners carefully. He hadn't been involved in any long-term affairs since right after college—and that disastrous time with Kayla Martin a few years ago, which he preferred to forget. He'd pretty much stuck to short-term affairs.

His family constantly reminded him he was the last Westmoreland bachelor living in Atlanta, but that was fine with him. Settling down and getting married were the furthest things from his mind. He was glad it wouldn't be an issue in his campaign, because his opponent, Orin Jeffries, was a long-term divorcé, and from what he'd heard, the man had no plans of ever remarrying.

Finally, he stood in front of room 1632. Only

pausing for a brief second, he reached out to open the door and then stopped when he remembered his mask. Glancing up and down the hall to make sure it was empty, he pulled the mask out of his pocket and put it on. Then, after drawing a deep breath, he opened the door.

The moment he opened the door, his eyes, that is, the portion of them that Olivia could see through his mask, met hers. They felt possessive, as if he was stamping ownership on her, when there was no way he could do that. He didn't know her true identity. He knew nothing about her other than that it seemed her need for him was just as elemental and strong as his need for her. It was a tangible thing, and she could feel it, all the way to her toes.

Yet there was something in the way he entered the room, not taking his eyes off her as he pushed the door closed behind him. And then giving the room only a cursory glance. Without a single word spoken between them, he swiftly crossed the room and drew her into his arms.

And kissed her.

There was nothing to be gained by any further talking, and they both knew it. And the moment his mouth touched hers, lightly at first, before devouring it with a hunger she felt deep in her belly, she moaned a silent acceptance of him and their night together.

This was sexual chemistry at its most potent. He was all passion, and she responded in kind. She kissed him, not with the same skill and experience he was leveling on her, but with a hunger that needed to be appeased, satisfied and explored.

The kiss intensified, and they both knew it wouldn't be enough to quench the desire waiting to be unleashed within them. Sensations were spreading through her, seeping deep into her bones and her senses. Urges that she had tried desperately to control were now threatening to consume her.

He reluctantly pulled his mouth away, and she watched as a sensuous smile touched his lips. "Tonight is worth everything," he whispered softly against her moist lips. "Not in my wildest imagination would I have thought of this happening."

Neither would I, Olivia thought. The masks were silly, but they had a profound purpose. So were the pretend names. With them, they were free to do what they pleased, without inhibitions or thought of consequences. If their paths were to cross again, after tonight, there would be no recognition, no recrimination and no need for denials. What happened in this hotel room tonight would stay in this hotel room tonight.

Reggie's gaze studied Olivia as he fought to catch his breath while doing the same for his senses. Kissing her, tasting her lips, had been like an obsession since the moment he'd laid eyes on her. The shape, texture and outline of her lips had a provocative effect on him. Some men were into the shape and size of a woman's breasts; others into her backside. He was definitely a lips man. The fullness of a pair, covered in lipstick or not, could induce a state of arousal in him. Just thinking of all the things he could do with them was enough to push him over the edge.

And then, losing control, he leaned down and kissed her again, and while his tongue dominated and played havoc with hers, he felt her loosen up, begin to relax in his arms. She wrapped her arms around his neck while her feminine curves so effortlessly pressed against him in a seamless melding of bodies. They fit together perfectly, naturally. There was nothing like having soft female limbs and a beautiful set of lips within reach, he thought.

The hand around her waist dipped, and he felt the curve of her backside through the gown she was wearing. A firm yet soft behind. He needed to get her out of her gown.

Pulling his mouth away, he swept her into his arms. At her startled gasp and with a swift glance, he met the eyes staring at him through the mask, and then his lips eased into a smile. So did hers. And with nothing left to be said, he walked to the bedroom.

Instead of placing her on the bed, he held her firmly in his arms and sat down on the love seat, adjusting her in his lap. She pulled in a deep breath and caught hold of the front of his jacket.

He smiled down at her. "Trust me. I'm not going to let you fall." She loosened her hold on him yet continued looking into his eyes, studying his features so intently that he couldn't help asking, "Like the part you can see?"

She smiled. "Yes. You have such an angular jaw. It speaks of strength and honesty. It also speaks of determination."

He raised a brow, wondering how Wonder Woman could tell those things about him from just studying his jaw. He stopped wondering when she reached out and her finger traced that same jaw that seemed to fascinate her.

"It's rigid, but not overbearing. Firm, but not domineering." She then smiled. "Yet I do see a few arrogant lines," she said, tapping the center of his jaw.

He had sat down with her in his arms, instead of placing her on the bed, so as not to rush things with her, to give her time to collect herself after their kisses. He refused to rush their lovemaking. For some reason, he wanted more, felt they deserved more. He was never one for small talk, but he figured he would take a stab at it. But now her touch was making it almost impossible not to touch. Not to undress her and give her the pleasure they both wanted. And then it came to him that the reason he was here with her had nothing to do with lust. He'd gone months without a woman warming his bed before. What was driving him more than anything was her appeal, her sexiness and his desire to mate with her in an intimate way. Only her.

He stood while cradling her tightly in his arms and moved toward the bed and gently placed her in the middle of it, handed her the rose and then he took a step back so she could be in the center of his vision. He wanted the full view of her.

Her shoulder-length hair was tousled around her face, at least the part of her face he could see. Her dress had risen when he'd placed her on the bed. She had to know it was in disarray and showing a great deal of flesh, but she didn't make a move to pull anything down, and he had no intention of suggesting she do so. So he looked, got his fill, saw the firmness of her thighs and the shapeliness of her knees. And he couldn't help but notice how the front of the dress was cut low, showing the top portion of her full and firm breasts. He was a lips man first and a breasts man second. As far as he was concerned, he had hit the jackpot.

Olivia wondered how long he would stand there and stare. But in a way, it reassured her that he liked what he saw. No man had taken the time to analyze her this way. She might as well make it worth his while. She placed the rose to one side and reached down and unclasped her shoes before slipping them off her feet. She tossed one and then the other to him. He caught them perfectly, and instead of dropping them to the floor, he tossed them onto the love seat they had just vacated.

She was surprised. He had recognized a pair of stilettos by Zanotti. They had been another whim of hers. Shoes were her passion, and she appreciated a man who knew quality and fine workmanship in a woman's shoes when he saw it. He moved up another notch in her book.

Now it was time to take off the rest. Because she never wore panties with panty hose, that would be easy. Instead of removing her panty hose last, she decided to take them off first. He wouldn't be expecting it, and the thought of catching him off guard stirred something inside of her. With his eyes still on her, she lifted her bottom off the bed slightly to ease down her panty hose, deliberately giving him a flash to let him know that once they were gone, there would not be any covering left. After she'd removed them, she rolled the hose up in a ball and tossed them to him. As with her shoes, he made a perfect catch, and then, while she watched him, he brought the balled-up nylon to his nose and took a whiff of her scent before placing it in the pocket of his jacket.

Her gaze had followed his hands, and now it moved back to his face. She saw the flaring of his nostrils and the tightening of his fists by his sides, and she saw something else. Something she had noted earlier, when he had walked across the room to her, but that now had grown larger. His erection. There was no doubt in her mind, unclothed and properly revealed, it would put Michelangelo's *David* to shame. Her artistic eye could even make out the shape of it through his pants. It was huge, totally developed, long and thick. And at the moment, totally aroused. That was evident by the way the erection was straining against the fly of his pants.

He shifted his stance. Evidently, he'd seen where her gaze had traveled, and she watched as his fingers went to the zipper of his tuxedo pants and slowly eased it down. She could only stare when, after bending to remove his shoes and socks, he stepped out of his pants, leaving his lower body clad only in a pair of sexy black briefs. She knew they were a designer pair; their shape, fit and support said it all. The man had thighs that were firm, hard and muscular. She didn't have to see his buns to know they were probably as tight as the rest of him. There was no need to ask if he worked out on occasion. The physical fitness of his body said it all.

And he looked sexy standing there, with a tux jacket and white shirt on top and a pair of sexy briefs covering his lower half. She figured he had decided to remove the clothes from the same part of his anatomy as she had. They were both undressing from the bottom up.

She held her breath, literally stopped breathing, when his hands then went to the waistband of his briefs. And while her gaze was glued to him, he slowly pulled the briefs down his legs.

Damn.

The man, thankfully, had no qualms about exposing himself, and for that she was grateful, because what her eyes were feasting on was definitely worth seeing. He was truly a work of art. And while her focus was contained, he went about removing the rest of his clothes. She wasn't aware of it until he stood before her, totally naked in all his glorious form.

Her gaze traveled the full length of his body once, twice, a total of three times before coming back to settle on his face. He was a naked, masked man, and she would love to have him pose for her as such. On canvas she would capture each and every detail of him. He was pure, one hundred percent male.

"It's your turn to take off the rest of your clothes, Wonder."

His words, deep and husky, floated around the already sexually charged room.

She forced her gaze from his thick shaft and moved it to his face as, on her knees, she reached behind herself and undid the hooks of her dress before pulling it over her head. It was simple, and she was naked, since she hadn't worn a bra.

Now he saw it all. And like she had earlier, his gaze moved to her lower part, zeroing in on the junction of her thighs. Suddenly she felt awkward. She wondered what he was thinking. She kept her body in great shape, and her Brazilian wax was obvious.

She met his gaze when he returned it to her face. She smiled. "I'm done."

"No, baby," he said in a tight and strained voice. "You haven't even got started."

Reggie pulled in a deep breath, meaning every word he'd just spoken. Never in his life had he been so hard and hot for a woman. Never had he wanted to eat one alive. As far as he was concerned, there would not be enough time tonight to do everything he wanted to do. So there was none to be wasted. But first…

"Is there anything you have an aversion to doing?" he felt the need to ask.

He watched how she lifted her gaze a moment, and then she said in a soft voice, "Yes. I'm not into bondage."

He chuckled. "Then it's a good thing I left my handcuffs at home." And because he saw the slight widening of her eyes, he smiled and said, "Hey, I'm just teasing. I would be crazy to tie your hands since I prefer you putting them all over me."

As far as Olivia was concerned, that was the

perfect invitation. She scooted close to the edge of the bed and reached out and splayed her hands across his chest. She smiled when she heard his sharp intake of breath. And she was fascinated by the way his muscles flexed beneath her hands and by the warmth of his skin beneath her fingers.

"You're into torture?" he asked huskily, his tone sounding somewhat strained.

"Why? Do you feel like you're being tortured?" she asked innocently, shifting one of her hands lower to his stomach.

"Yes." His answer was short and precise. His breathing seemingly impaired.

"You haven't seen anything yet, Jack Sprat."

And then her hand dropped to that part of him she'd become fascinated with from the moment she'd seen it. It was large, heavy and, for tonight, it was hers. Her hand closed up, contracted and then closed up again, liking the feel of holding it, stroking it.

Breathing at full capacity, Reggie could no longer handle what his mystery woman was doing to him and pulled back and reached down for his pants to retrieve a condom packet from his wallet. Ripping the packet with his teeth, he proceeded to put the condom on.

He glanced up to see her lying back on the bed, smiling at him, fully aware of the state she'd pushed him to. He moved so quickly, it caught her off guard, and then he was there with her in the bed, pinning her beneath him on the coverlet and immediately taking her mouth captive, devouring it like he intended to devour her. And when he pulled back, he moved down to her breasts, taking the nipples in his mouth, doing all kinds of things to them with his tongue until she cried out. She pleaded with him to stop, because she couldn't take any more.

But he definitely wasn't through with her yet. Intent on proving that she wasn't the only one with hands that could torture, he used his knee to spread her legs. He then settled between them, determined to fit his erection in the place where it was supposed to be.

There was so much more he wanted to do—devour her breasts, lick her skin all over—but at that moment, the one thing he had to do before his brain exploded with need was get inside of her.

He pulled his mouth away from her breasts, and breathing hard, he stared down at her, determined to see what he could of her eyes through the mask. "This is crazy," he said, almost choking for both breath and control of the words.

"Might be," she said, just as short of breath. "But it's the best craziness I've ever experienced. Let's not stop now."

He stared at her. "You sure?"

She stared back. "Positive."

And with their gazes locked, he entered her.

He felt her small spasms before he even got into the hilt, and when her inner muscles clenched him, he pressed deeper inside of her. She was tight, but he could feel her opening wider for him, like a bloom. "That's it. Relax, let go and let me in," he said.

And as if her body was his to command, it continued to open, adjust, until it was a perfect fit and curved around him like a glove. And at that moment, while buried deep inside of her, he just had to taste her lips again. He leaned forward, took her mouth and began swallowing every deep, wrenching moan that she made.

And then he began moving back and forth inside of her, thrusting, then retreating, then repeating the process all over again, each thrust aimed with perfect accuracy at her erogenous zone. He lifted her hips, and she dug her fingertips deep into his shoulders and cried out with each stroke he took.

It was at that moment that he actually felt her body explode. Then the sensations that had rippled through her slammed through him as well. He threw his head back; and he felt the muscles in his neck pop; and he breathed in deep, pulling in her scent, which filled the air.

Shudders rammed through him, and he squeezed his eyes shut as his body exploded. His orgasm came with the force of a tidal wave, and he continued to thrust inside her as his groans mingled with her cries of pleasure. And with their bodies fully engaged, their minds unerringly connected, together they left Earth and soared into the clouds as unadulterated pleasure consumed them.

"I need to leave," she said softly.

Reggie turned his head on the pillow and looked over at Wonder. He doubted he could move. He could barely breathe. It was close to morning. They'd made love all night long. As soon as they had ended one session, they'd been quick and eager to start another.

He knew she had to leave. So did he. But he didn't want their one and only night together to end. "You do know there is no reason why we can't—"

She quickly turned toward him and placed a finger on his lips. "Yes, there is. I can't tell you my true identity. It could hurt someone."

He frowned. She wasn't wearing a ring, so quite naturally, he had assumed she wasn't married. What if she...

As if reading his mind, she said, "I don't have a husband. I don't even have a boyfriend."

"Then who?" he asked quickly, trying to understand why they couldn't bring their masquerade to an end. He probably had more to lose than she, because his campaign for the Senate officially began Monday.

"I can't say. This has to be goodbye—"

Before the words were completely out of her mouth, he reached out and pulled her into his arms, knowing this would be the last time he would kiss the lips he had grown so attached to.

Moments later he released her mouth, refusing to say goodbye. She wiggled out of his arms and began re-dressing. He watched her do so, getting turned on all over again.

"I'm getting money out of the ATM to pay for the room," she informed him.

He frowned at her words. "No, you're not."

"I must. It was my idea for us to come here," she said.

"Doesn't matter. Everything has been taken care of, so they won't take any money from you at the front desk. Last night is on me, and I don't regret one minute of spending it with you."

Olivia slipped back into her shoes and gazed across the room at him. He was lying in bed, on top of the covers. Naked. So immensely male. "And I don't regret anything, either," she said, meaning every word. She was tempted to do as he wanted— cross the room, remove his mask and remove hers as well—but she couldn't. She couldn't even trust herself to kiss him goodbye. It had to be a clean break for both of them. "And you sure you don't want me to pay for the room?" she asked.

"Yes, I'm sure."

"At least let me give you something toward it and—"

"No," he said, declining her offer.

She didn't know how much time passed while they just stared at each other. But she knew she had to leave. "I have to go now," she said, as if convincing herself of that.

He shifted on the bed to take the rose, and offered it to her. She closed the short distance between them to retrieve it. "At least let me walk you to the door," he said.

She shook her head. "No. I'll see myself out."

And then she quickly walked out of the bedroom.

Reggie pulled himself up in the bed when he heard the sound of the hotel door closing. He sat on the edge of the bed, suddenly feeling a sense of loss that touched his very soul and not understanding how such a thing was possible.

He stood up to put on his clothes, and it was then that he snatched off the mask. It had served its purpose. He reached for his shirt and tie and noticed something glittering on the carpet. He reached down and picked it up. It was one of the diamond earrings that she had been wearing.

He folded the earring in the palm of his hand. He knew at that very moment that if he had to turn Atlanta upside down, he would find his Wonder Woman.

He would find her, and he would keep her.

Three

"So, Libby, how was the party?"

Olivia, who had been so entrenched in the memories of the night before, hadn't noticed her father standing at the bottom of the stairs. She glanced down at him and smiled. "It was simply wonderful." He didn't need to know that she was speaking not of the party per se but of the intimate party she'd gone to at the Saxon Hotel, with her mystery man.

It had been just before six in the morning when she slipped into her father's home, and knowing he was an early riser, she had dashed up the stairs and showered. She had also put in a call to Terrence, leaving a message on his cell phone that it was okay to delete the text message she had sent to him the night before. And then she had climbed into bed. By the time her head had hit the pillow in her own bed, she had heard her father moving around.

She had enjoyed the best sleep in years. She had awakened to a hungry stomach, and the last person she had expected to meet when she took the stairs to go pillaging in the kitchen was her father. Typically, after early morning church services on Sunday, he hit the country club with his buddies for a game of golf. So why was he still here?

Orin met his daughter on the bottom stair and gave her a hug. "I'm glad you enjoyed yourself. I felt kind of bad that I couldn't attend the ball with you, but I did have to work on that speech."

She looked up at him and, not for the first time, thought that he was definitely a good-looking man, and she was glad he took care of himself by eating right and staying active. "No problem, Dad."

Not wanting him to ask for details about the party, she quickly asked a question of her own. "So why are you home and not out on the golf course?"

He smiled as he tucked her arm in his and escorted her to the kitchen. "Cathy threatened me with dire consequences today if I left before she got the chance to come over and go over my speech."

Olivia smiled but didn't say anything for a moment. Cathy Bristol had been her father's private secretary for almost fifteen years, and Olivia couldn't help but wonder when her father would wake up and realize the woman was in love with him. Olivia had figured it out when she was in her teens, and when she'd gotten older had asked her brothers about it. Like her dad, they'd been clueless. But at least Duan and Terrence had opened their eyes even if her father hadn't. Cathy was a forty-eight-year-old widow who had lost her husband over eighteen years ago, when he died in a car accident, leaving her with two sons to raise.

"So when is Cathy coming? I'd love to see her."

Her father smiled. "Around noon. I'm treating her to lunch here first before I put her to work."

"To review your speech?"

"Yes," he said when they reached the kitchen and he sat down at the table. "She's good at editing things and giving her opinion. As this is my first speech, I want to impress those who hear it. It will be one of those forums in which all the candidates speak."

Olivia nodded as she grabbed an apple out of the fruit bowl on the table and sat down across from him.

Orin frowned. "Surely that's not all you're having for breakfast."

"Afraid so," she said before biting into her apple.

"You're so thin," he pointed out. "You should eat more."

Olivia could only smile. There was no way she could tell her father that she had eaten quite a lot last night. After making love several times, they had ordered room service, eaten until their stomachs were full and then gone back to bed to make love some more.

Deciding to get her father off the subject of her weight, she said, "So, tell me something about this guy who has the audacity to run against my father."

Orin leaned back in his chair. "He's one of those Westmorelands. Prominent family here in Atlanta. He's young, in his early thirties, and owns an accounting firm."

Olivia nodded. She recalled the name, and if she wasn't mistaken, Duan and Terrence had gone to school with some of them. They were a huge family. "So what's his platform? How do the two of you differ?"

"On a number of issues, we're in agreement. The main thing we differ on is whether or not Georgia can support another state-financed university. He thinks we can, and I don't. We have a number of fine colleges and universities in this area. Why on earth would we need another one? Besides, he's inexperienced."

Olivia couldn't help but smile at that, because her father didn't have any political experience, either. In fact, she and her brothers had been shocked when he'd announced he was running for a political office. The only thing they could come up with as to the reason was that his good friend and golfing buddy Senator Albert Reed was retiring and wanted someone to replace him whom he knew and could possibly influence. Not that her father was easily influenced, but he was known to give in under a good argument, without fully standing his ground.

"And young Westmoreland will run on his name recognition since he has a couple of celebrities in the family. One of his cousins is a motorcycle racer, and another is an author."

And your son just happens to be a very well-known former NFL player, she wanted to say. Who you have called upon to appear at a couple of rallies. So you are just as bad.

Olivia said nothing but listened as she took another bite of her apple. At least she tried to listen. More than once her mind took a sharp turn, and she found her thoughts drifting to breath-stopping memories of the tall, dark and handsome man she had met and spent a wonderful night with. She could vividly recall his kisses and the way he had been methodically slow and extremely thorough each time he'd taken her mouth in his, eating away at her lips, unrestrained, unhurried and not distracted.

And there were the times his mouth had touched her everywhere, blazing a trail from her nape to her spine, then all over her chest, tasting her nipples and making her intensely aware of all her hidden passion—passion he'd been able to wrench from her.

The only bad thing about last night was the fact that she had lost one of the diamond earrings she had purchased a year ago in Paris. The earrings had been a gift to herself when she landed her dream job. She would love to get it back, but knew that wouldn't be happening. But she would be the first to admit that the night spent in her one-time lover's arms had been worth the loss.

The ringing of the doorbell claimed her attention and brought her back to the present.

"That must be Cathy," Orin said. He quickly rose from the table and headed to the front door.

Olivia studied her father and couldn't do anything but shake her head. He seemed awfully excited about Cathy's arrival. Olivia couldn't help wondering if perhaps her father had finally awakened and smelled the coffee and just wasn't aware he'd been sniffing the aroma. She had been around her brothers long enough to know that when it came to matters of the heart, men had a tendency to be slow.

She turned in her seat when she heard a feminine voice, Cathy's voice. Olivia smiled when she saw the one woman she felt would be good for her father and again wondered why her father hadn't asked Cathy to be his escort for some of these functions. Cathy was very pretty, and Olivia thought, as she glanced at the two of them walking into the kitchen, that they complemented each other well.

Brent Fairgate waved his hand back and forth in front of Reggie's face. "Hey, man, are you with us, or are you somewhere in la-la land?"

Reggie blinked, and then his gaze focused on the man standing in front of him, before shifting to the woman standing beside him, Pam Wells. Brent had hired Pam as a strategist on a consulting basis.

"Sorry," he said, since there was no use denying they hadn't had his attention. "My mind drifted elsewhere for a moment." There was no way he was going to tell Brent that he was reliving the memories of the prior night. Brent was the most focused man that Reggie knew. Reggie was well aware that Brent wanted him to be just as focused.

"Okay. Then let's go back over the layout for tomorrow," Brent said, handing him a folder filled with papers. "The luncheon is at the Civic Center, and both you and Jeffries will be speaking. The order will be determined by a flip of a coin. You got the speech down pat. Just make sure you turn on your charm. Jeffries will be doing likewise. Without coming right out and saying it, you will have to make everyone see you as the voice of change. You will have to portray Jeffries as more of the same, someone who represents the status quo."

"Okay. Give me some personal info on Jeffries, other than he's the Holy Terror's father," Reggie said.

Early in his professional football career, Terrence Jeffries had been nicknamed the "Holy Terror" by sportscasters. Reggie understood that Terrence was now a very successful businessman living in the Florida Keys.

"He also has another son, who's a couple years older than the Holy Terror," Pam replied. "He used to be on the Atlanta police force, but now he owns a private investigation company. He's low-key and definitely not in the public eye like Terrence."

Reggie nodded. "That's it? Two sons?"

Pam shook her head. "There's also a daughter, the youngest. She's twenty-seven. An artist who lives in Paris. I understand she's returned home for the campaign."

Reggie lifted a brow. "Why?"

Pam smiled. "To act as her father's escort for all the fund-raisers he'll be expected to attend. From what I understand, he hasn't dated a lot since his wife up and left him."

Reggie frowned. "And when was that?"

"Over twenty-something years ago. He raised his kids as a single father," said Pam.

Reggie nodded, immediately admiring the man for taking on such a task. He was blessed to have both of his parents still living and still married to each other. He couldn't imagine otherwise. He had heard his siblings and cousins talk about the hard work that went into parenting, so he admired any person who did it solo.

"As you know, Orin Jeffries is a corporate attorney at Nettleton Industries. He's worked for them for over thirty years. And he's almost twenty-five years older than you. He'll likely flaunt the age difference and his greater experience," Brent added.

Reggie smiled. "I'm sure that he will."

"Do you need me to look over your speech for tomorrow?" Brent asked.

Reggie met his friend's gaze. "I haven't written it yet." Concern touched Brent's features, and not for the first time, Reggie thought his best friend worried too much.

"But I thought you were going to do it last night, right after you came home from the Firemen's Masquerade Ball," Brent said.

Reggie sighed. There was no way he was going to mention that he hadn't made it home from the ball until this morning, because he had made a pit stop at the Saxon Hotel. Actually, it had been more than a pit stop. The word *quickie* in no way described what he and Wonder Woman had done practically all through the night. They had refused to be rushed.

Before Brent could chew him out, Reggie said, "I'll do it as soon as the two of you leave. If you want to drop by later and look it over, then feel free to do so."

A stern look appeared on Brent's face. "And don't think that I won't."

Reggie rolled his eyes. "Just don't return before six this evening."

Brent raised a brow. "Why?"

"Because I need to take a nap."

Brent chuckled. "You never take naps."

Determined not to explain anything, Reggie said, "I know, but today I definitely need one."

As soon as Pam and Brent left, Reggie called and checked in with his parents. Usually on Sunday he would drop by for dinner, and he didn't want his mother to worry when he didn't make an appearance.

After convincing Sarah Westmoreland that he was not coming down with a flu bug and that he just needed to rest, he was ready to end the call, but she kept him on the phone longer than he'd planned to give him a soup recipe...like he would actually take the time to make it. Not that she figured he would. She was just hoping he had a lady friend available to do his bidding.

He couldn't help but smile as he climbed the stairs to his bedroom. His mother's one wish in life was to live to see her six sons all married and herself and his father surrounded by grandchildren. A bout with breast cancer a few years ago had made her even more determined to see each one of her sons happily married.

Her dream had come true—almost. Jared's recent announcement that he and his wife, Dana, would become parents in the fall meant that all of James and Sarah Westmoreland's sons—with the exception of him—were married and either had kids or were expecting them. Quade had blown everyone away with his triplets. But then multiple births ran in the Westmoreland family.

When he reached his bedroom, he began stripping off his clothes, remembering when he had stripped for an audience of one the night before. He had been aware that Wonder Woman's eyes had been directed on him while he'd taken off each piece...the same way his eyes had been on her.

As he slid between the covers, he promised himself that once he woke up, he would have slept off the memories and would be focused on the present again. That morning he'd thought about trying to find his mystery woman, and he still intended to do that, but he owed it to Brent and his campaign staff to stay focused and put all his time and energy into winning this election.

But still...

He thought about the lone earring he had in his dresser drawer. On the way into the office, he would stop by Jared's favorite jewelry store, Garbella Jewelers, to see if they could possibly tell him anything about the earring, like who had made it and, possibly, from which store it had been purchased. Checking on something like that shouldn't take too long and wouldn't make him lose focus.

As he felt himself drifting off to sleep, his mind was flooded with more memories. He wondered how long this fascination, this mind-reeling, gut-wrenching obsession with his mystery woman, would last.

He wasn't sure, but he intended to enjoy it while it did.

Olivia sat in the chair across the room, and her observant eye zeroed in on her father and Cathy. She tried not to chuckle when she noticed how they would look at each other when the other one wasn't watching. Boy, they had it bad, but in a way, she was glad. Sooner or later, her father would realize that Cathy was the best thing to ever happen to him. Even now, after working as his secretary for over fifteen years, their relationship was still professional. She knew in time that would change, and she would do her part to help it along.

"Dad?"

Orin looked up from his seat behind his desk and glanced over at her. Cathy was standing next to his chair. They'd had their heads together while Cathy critiqued his speech. "Yes, sweetheart?"

"Why did you send for me to be your escort for

all these fund-raising events when you had Cathy right here?"

As if on cue, Cathy blushed, and her father's jaw dropped as if he was surprised she would ask something like that. Before he could pick up his jaw to respond, Cathy spoke, stammering through her explanation.

"T-there's no way Orin can do something like that. I'm his secretary."

Olivia smiled. "Oh." What she was tempted to say was that secretary or no secretary, Cathy was also the woman her father couldn't keep his eyes off. She couldn't wait until she talked to Duan and Terrence.

And then, as if by luck or fate, since it also seemed to be on cue, her cell phone rang, and when she stood and pulled it out of her back jeans pocket, she saw the call was from Terrence.

Knowing it was best to take the call privately, she said, "Excuse me a moment while I take this." She quickly walked out of the room and closed the office door behind her.

"Yes, Terrence?"

"What the hell is going on with you, Libby? Why did you text me from an unknown number and then call this morning and ask that the text be deleted?"

Olivia nervously licked her lips. One thing about Terrence was that he would ask questions, but if she gave him a reason that sounded remotely plausible, he would let it go, whereas Duan would continue to ask questions.

"Last night I went to this charity party in Dad's place and met a guy. He asked me to follow him to a nightclub in Stone Mountain, and I did, but I felt I should take precautions."

"That was a good idea. Smart girl. So how was the club?"

"Umm, nice, but it didn't compare to Club Hurricane," she said, knowing he would like to hear that she thought the nightclub he owned in the Keys was at the top of the list.

"You're even smarter than I thought. So how's Dad? He hasn't dropped out of this Senate race yet?"

Olivia smiled. Terrence and Duan were taking bets that sooner or later, when Orin Jeffries got a taste of what real politics were like, he would call it quits. At first she had agreed with them, but now she wasn't so sure. "I don't know, Terrence. I think he's going all the way with this one."

"Umm, that's interesting. I still think Reed pushed Dad into running for his own benefit. I'm going to give Duan a call. We might need to talk to Dad about this."

"You might be too late. The first forum is tomorrow, and he's giving a speech. He's been working on it for two days. The only good thing coming out of all this is that he and Cathy are working together," she said.

"Libby, they always work closely together. She's his secretary."

"Yes, but they are working closely together in a different way, on issues other than Nettleton Industries business. In fact, she's over here now."

She could hear her brother chuckle. "Still determined to play Cupid, are you?"

"I might as well while I'm here, since I have nothing else to do." She thought of Jack Sprat. She had been tempted earlier to pull out her art pad and do some sketches to pass the time. She had thought about drawing her mystery man with the mask and then playing around to see if she could draw sketches of how she imagined he might look without the mask. She had eventually talked herself out of it.

"Well, I'll be coming home in a couple of weeks, so stay out of trouble until then, sport."

She laughed. "I can't make you any promises, but I'll try."

Four

Brent had given his speech a thumbs-up, so Reggie felt confident it would go over well. He walked around the luncheon reception, greeting all those who had arrived to attend the forum. This would be the first of several gatherings designed to give voters a chance to learn each candidate's agenda. He had met Orin Jeffries when he'd first arrived and thought the older man was a likable guy.

A number of his family members were present and a number of his friends as well. These were people who believed in him, supported him and were counting on him to make changes to some of the present policies.

A career in politics had been the last thing on his mind and had never been his heart's desire, until recently. He'd become outraged at the present senators' refusal to recognize the state's need for an additional college. More and more young people were making the decision to acquire higher learning, and the lower tuition costs of state universities compared to private universities were a key factor in the process. It was hard enough for students to get the funds they needed to go to college, but when they were refused entrance into schools because of campus overcrowding, that was unacceptable. Anyone who wanted a college education should be able to get one. Georgia needed another state-run college, and he was willing to fight for it.

The University of Georgia was the oldest public university in the state and had been established by an act of the Georgia General Assembly over two centuries ago. Just as there had been a need for greater educational opportunities then, there was a need now. In fact, land had been donated for that very purpose ten years ago. Now some lawmakers were trying to use a loophole in the land grant to appropriate the land to build a recreation area—a park that would be largely composed of a golf course.

Reggie was aware that getting elected would only be the first hurdle. Once he got in the Senate, he would then have the job of convincing his fellow lawmakers of the need for an additional state university as well.

He glanced at his watch. In less than ten minutes, lunch would be served, and then halfway through lunch, each person seeking office would get an opportunity to speak. There were about eight candidates in attendance.

Deciding he needed to switch his focus for a moment, he thought about his visit to Garbella Jewelers that morning. Mr. Garbella's assessment of the earring was that it was a fine piece of craftsmanship. The diamonds were real and of good quality. He doubted the piece had been purchased in this country. He thought the way the diamonds were set was indicative of European jewelry making. Mr. Garbella had gone on to say that the pair had cost a lot of money. After visiting with the jeweler, Reggie was more determined than ever to find his Wonder Woman and return the missing earring to her.

Quade and his cousin Cole, who'd both recently retired—Quade from a top security job with the government and Cole from the Texas Rangers— had joined forces to start a network of security companies, some of which would include private investigation. He wondered if they would be interested in taking him on as their first client.

He looked at his watch again before glancing

across the room and meeting Brent's eye. He had less than ten minutes to mingle, and then everyone would be seated for lunch. He hated admitting it, but he felt in his element. Maybe a political career was his calling, after all.

Olivia waited until just moments before the luncheon was to begin to make an entrance and join her father. According to his campaign manager, Marc Norris, her entrance was part of a co-ordinated strategy. He wanted her to ease into the room and work one side of it while her father worked the other. Subtle yet thorough.

When he had mentioned his strategy that morning while joining Olivia and her father for breakfast, she had gotten annoyed that the man assumed she didn't have any common sense. Evidently, Norris doubted she could hold her own during any discussion. But not to cause any problems, she had decided to keep her opinions to herself.

She saw noticeable interest in her from the moment she stepped into the room. Most people knew that Orin Jeffries had a daughter, but a number of them had forgotten or shoved the fact to the back of their mind in the wake of his two well-known sons. Practically everybody in the country knew of the Holy Terror, whether they were football enthusiasts or not. Since retiring from football, Terrence had been known for his work in a number of high-

profile charities. He also commented on a pop-
ular radio talk show, *Sports Talk,* in South Florida,
which might go into syndication the next year.
Duan had made the national headlines a few years
before, when his undercover work as a detective
had resulted in the exposure of a couple of un-
savory individuals who'd been intent on bringing
organized crime to Georgia.

But it didn't bother her in the least that her
brothers' good deeds had somehow made people
forget about her. Besides, she hadn't lived in this
country in four years, returning only on occasion
to visit, mainly around the holidays.

She began mingling, introducing herself as Orin
Jeffries's daughter, and actually got a kick out of
seeing first surprise and then acknowledgment on
many faces. One such incident was taking place
now.

"Why, Olivia, how good it is to see you again.
It's been a while since you've been back home. But
I do remember you now. You must be extremely
proud of your father and brothers."

"Yes, I am, Mrs. Hancock, and how is Beau? I
understand he's doing extremely well. You must be
proud of him."

She watched the older woman's eyes light up as
she went into a spiel about her son. She was a
proud mother. Olivia knew Beau from school. Unless he had changed over the years, Beau Hancock

was an irrefutable jerk. He'd thought he was the gift to every girl at Collinshill High School.

She glanced down at her watch. She had ten minutes left before everyone would take their seats for lunch. She had called the Saxon Hotel on the off chance that someone from housekeeping had come across her diamond earring and turned it in. That hadn't been the case. A part of her was disappointed that it had not been.

There was still one section of the room she needed to cover. Mrs. Hancock, in singing Beau's praises, had taken up quite a bit of her time. Now she was again making her way through the crowds, speaking to everyone, as Norris had suggested.

"You're doing a marvelous job working the room," Senator Reed whispered. The older man had suddenly appeared by her side.

She forced a smile. For some reason, she'd never cared for him. "Thanks."

She had already met several of the candidates since entering the room, but she had yet to meet the man who would be her father's real competition, Reggie Westmoreland.

As she continued mingling and heading to the area where Reggie Westmoreland was supposedly rubbing elbows with the crowd, her curiosity about the man who opposed her father couldn't help but be piqued. She started to ask Senator Reed about him but changed her mind. The senator's opinion wouldn't be the most valuable.

"You look nice, Olivia."

She glanced up at the senator, who seemed determined to remain by her side. He was a few years older than her father, and for some reason, he had always made her feel uncomfortable.

"Thanks, Senator." She refrained from saying that he also looked nice, which he did. Like her father, he was a good-looking man for his age, but Senator Reed always had an air of snobbery about him, like he was born with too low expectations of others.

"It was my suggestion that your father send for you." When she stopped walking and glanced at him, with a raised brow, he added, "He was in a dilemma, and I thought bringing you home to be his escort was the perfect answer."

She bit back a retort, that bringing her home had not been the perfect answer. Being in that dilemma might have prompted her dad to ask Cathy to attend some of those functions with him. No telling how things would have taken off from there if the senator hadn't butted in.

She was about to open her mouth, to tell Senator Reed that her father was old enough to think for himself, when, all of a sudden, for no reason at all, she pulled in a quick breath. She glanced up ahead, and no more than four feet in front of her, there stood a man with his back to her.

The first thing she noticed about him was his height. He was taller then the men he was talking to. And there was something about his particular height, and the way his head tilted at an angle as he listened to what one of the men was saying, that held her spellbound.

He was dressed in a suit, and she could only admire how it fit him. The broadness of his shoulders and the tapering of his waist sent a feeling of familiarity through her. She stopped walking momentarily and composed herself, not understanding what was happening to her.

"Is anything wrong, Olivia?"

She glanced up at Senator Reed and saw concern in his eyes. She knew she couldn't tell him what she was thinking. There was no way she could voice her suspicions to anyone.

She needed to go somewhere to pull herself together, to consider the strong possibility that the man standing not far away was her Jack Sprat. Or could it be that she was so wrapped up in the memories of that night that she was quick to assume that any man of a tall stature who possessed broad shoulders had to be her mystery man?

"Olivia?"

Instead of saying anything, she shifted her gaze from the senator to look again at the man, whose back was still to her. It was at that precise moment that he slowly turned around, and his gaze settled on her. In a quick second, she pulled in a sharp breath as she scanned his face, and her gaze settled on a firm jaw that had an angular plane. Her artist's eye also picked up other things, and they were things others would probably not notice—the stark symmetry of his face, which was clear with or without a mask, the shape of his head and the alignment of his ears from his cheeks. These were things she recognized.

Things she remembered.

And she knew, without a doubt, that she was staring into the face of the man whom she had spent the night with on Saturday. The man whose body had given her hours upon hours of immeasurable pleasure. And impossible as it seemed— because they'd kept their masks in place the entire time—she had a feeling from the way he was staring back at her just as intently as she was staring at him that he had recognized her, too.

"Olivia?"

She broke eye contact with the stranger to gaze up at the senator. The man was becoming annoying, but at the moment, he was the one person who could tell her exactly what she needed to know. "Senator Reed, that guy up there, the one who turned around to look at me. Who is he?"

The senator followed her gaze and frowned deeply. "The two of you had to meet eventually. That man, young lady, is the enemy."

She swallowed deeply before saying, "The enemy?"

"Yes, the enemy. He's the man that's opposing your father in his bid for the Senate."

Olivia's head began spinning before the senator could speak his next words.

"That, my dear," the senator went on to say, "is Reggie Westmoreland."

It was her.

Reggie knew it with every breath he took. Her lips were giving her away. And he wasn't sure what part of him was recognizable to her, but he knew just as sure as they were standing there, staring at each other, that they were as intimately familiar to each other as any two people could be.

It was strange. He'd been standing here with Brent, his brother Jared, his cousins Dare and Thorn, and Thorn's wife, Tara. They'd all been listening to Thorn, a nationally known motorcycle builder and racer, who was telling them about an order he'd received to build a bike for actor Matt Damon. Then, all of a sudden, he'd felt a strange sensation, followed by a stirring in the lower part of his gut.

He had turned around, and he'd looked straight into her face. His Wonder Woman.

He couldn't lay claim to recognizing any of her other facial features, but her lips were a dead giveaway. Blatantly sensual, he had kissed them, tongued them, licked them and tasted them to his heart's content. He knew the shape of them in his sleep, knew their texture, knew what part of them was so sensitive that when he'd touched her there, she had moaned.

She looked totally stunning in the stylish skirt and blouse she was wearing. The outfit complemented her figure. Even if he hadn't met her before, he would be trying his best to do so now. Out of his peripheral vision, he noted a number of men looking at her, and he understood why. She was gorgeous.

He lost control, and his feet began moving toward her.

"Reggie, where are you going?" Brent asked.

He didn't respond, because he truly didn't know what he could say. He continued walking until he came to a stop directly in front of the senator and the woman. The senator, he noted, was frowning. The woman's gaze hadn't left his. She seemed as entranced as he was.

He found his voice to say, "Good afternoon, Senator Reed. It's good seeing you again."

It was a lie, and he realized the senator knew it, but he didn't care. Approaching him would force the man to make introductions, and if it took a lie, then so be it.

"Westmoreland, I see you've decided to go through with it," replied the senator.

Reggie gave the man a smile that didn't quite

reach his eyes. "Of course." He then shifted his gaze back to the woman. The senator would be outright rude not to make an introduction, and one thing Reggie did know about the senator was that he believed in following proper decorum.

"And let me introduce you to Olivia Jeffries. Olivia, this is Reggie Westmoreland," the senator said.

At the mention of her name, Reggie's mind went into a tailspin. "Jeffries?" he replied.

"Yes," the senator said as a huge, smug smile touched his lips. "Jeffries. She's Orin Jeffries's daughter, who is visiting from Paris and will remain here during the duration of the campaign."

Reggie nodded as his eyes once again settled on Olivia. He then reached out his hand. "Olivia, it's nice meeting you. I'm sure your father is excited about having you home."

"Thank you," replied Olivia.

They both felt it the moment their hands touched, and they both knew it. It was those same feelings that had driven them to leave the party on Saturday night and to go somewhere to be alone, with the sole purpose of getting intimately connected. Reggie opened his mouth to say something, and then a voice from the microphone stopped him.

"Everyone is asked to take a seat so lunch can be served. Your table number is located on your ticket."

"It was nice meeting you, Mr. Westmoreland," Olivia said, not sure what else to say at the moment.

She honestly had thought she would not see him again, not this soon, not ever. And now that he knew their predicament—that she was the daughter of the man who was his opponent in this political race—she hoped that he would accept the inevitable. Nothing had changed. Even with their identities exposed, there could never be anything between them beyond what had happened Saturday night.

"It was nice meeting you as well, Ms. Jeffries," said Reggie. And then he did something that was common among Frenchmen but rare with Americans. Bending slightly, he lifted her hand to his lips and kissed it before turning and walking away.

Five

Olivia found that every time she lifted her fork to her mouth, her gaze would automatically drift to the next table, the one where Reggie Westmoreland was sitting. And each time, unerringly, their gazes would meet.

After their introduction, she had excused herself to the senator, smiling and saying she needed to go to the ladies' room. Once there she had taken a deep breath. It was a wonder she hadn't passed out. With his mask in place, Reggie Westmoreland had been handsome. Without his mask, he took her breath away. While standing in front of him, she'd had to tamp down her emotions and the sensations flowing through her.

His eyes were very dark, almost chocolate, and their shape, which she had been denied seeing on Saturday night, was almond, beneath thick brows. It had taken everything in her power to force her muscles to relax. And when he had taken her hand and kissed the back of it before walking off, she'd thought she would swoon right then and there.

"Libby, are you okay? You've barely touched your meal," her father said, interrupting her thoughts.

She glanced over to him and smiled. "Yes, Daddy, I'm fine."

"Westmoreland is the cause of it," said Senator Reed, jumping in. "She met him right before we took our seats. He probably gave her an upset stomach."

Her father frowned. "Was he rude to you, sweetheart?" he asked, with deep concern tinged with anger.

She was opening her mouth to assure her father that Reggie hadn't been rude when Senator Reed said, "He was quite taken with her, Orin."

She ignored the senator's comment, thinking that he didn't know the half of it. Instead, she answered her father. "No, he wasn't rude, Dad. In fact, although we spoke only briefly, I thought he was rather nice." She smiled. "Quite the charmer."

"The enemy is never nice or charming, Olivia. Remember that," the senator said, speaking to her like she was a child. "I strongly suggest that during this campaign, you stay away from him."

She was opening her mouth to tell the senator that she truly didn't give a royal damn about what he would strongly suggest when her father spoke.

"You don't have to worry about Libby, Al. She's a smart girl. She would never get mixed up with the likes of Westmoreland."

The likes of Westmoreland? Was there something about Reggie that her father and the senator knew but that she didn't? she wondered. Granted, that might be true, since she had arrived in the country on Friday. But still, she heard intense dislike in her father's voice and pondered the reason for it. Did it have to do only with the campaign, or was there more? Marc Norris was the only other person at their table, and he wasn't saying anything. But then Norris didn't look like the type to gossip. She didn't know him well. In fact, she had just met him on Friday evening.

"Well, if I didn't know better, I'd think Olivia and Westmoreland had met before," replied Senator Reed.

The senator's words almost made her drop her fork. She had to tighten her grip on it. She thought about Reggie. Had their reaction to each other been that obvious?

There was a lag in the conversation at the table, and she knew from the brief moment of silence that the men were waiting for her to respond one

way or the other. So she did. "Then it's a good
thing that you know better, Senator, isn't it?"

She said the words so sweetly, there was no
way that he or anyone else could tell if she was
being sincere or smart-alecky. Before any further
conversation could take place, one of the sponsors
of the event got up and went to the podium to
announce that the speeches were about to begin.

"Okay, Reggie. What's going on with you and
that woman at the other table? The one you can't
seem to keep your eyes off," Brent said in a whisper as he leaned close to Reggie.

Reggie lifted a brow. "What makes you think
something is going on?"

Brent chuckled. "I have eyes. I can see. You do
know she's Jeffries's daughter."

Reggie leaned back in his chair. He couldn't eat
another mouthful, although he hadn't eaten much.
He was still trying to recover from the fact that he
and his mystery woman had officially met. "Yes, the
senator introduced us. And grudgingly, I might add.
He didn't seem too happy to do so," Reggie said.

"Figures. He probably wants her for himself." At
Reggie's surprised look, Brent went on to explain.
"Reed is into young women big-time. I once dated
someone who worked at his office. He tried coming
on to her several times, and she ended up quitting
when the old man wouldn't give up no matter how

many times she tried turning him off. The man takes sexual harassment to a whole new level."

Reggie's jaw tightened. The thought that the senator could be interested in Olivia, even remotely, made his blood boil. "But he's friends with her father."

"And that's supposed to mean something?" Brent countered, trying to keep his voice low. "I guess it would mean something to honorable men, but Reed is not honorable. We don't have a term-limit law here, so it makes you wonder why he isn't seeking another term. Rumor has it that he was given a choice to either step down or have his business—namely, his affairs with women half his age—spread across the front pages of the newspapers. I guess since he's still married and his wife is wealthier than he is, although she's bedridden, he didn't want that."

Reggie shook his head. "Well, he shouldn't concern himself with Olivia Jeffries."

"And why is that?"

Reggie didn't say anything for fear of saying too much. In the end, he didn't have to respond, because it was his turn to speak.

"You gave a nice speech, Dad. You did a wonderful job," Olivia said once she and her father got home.

"Yes, but so did Westmoreland," Orin said, heading for the kitchen. "He tried to make me look like someone who doesn't support higher education."

"But only because you are against any legislation to build another state university," she reminded him.

"We have enough colleges, Libby."

She decided to back away from the conversation because she didn't agree with her father on this issue. The last thing she wanted was to get into an argument with him about Reggie Westmoreland and his speech. If nothing else, she had reached the conclusion at dinner that neither her father nor the senator wanted her to get involved in any way with the competition.

She glanced at her watch. "I think I'm going to change and then go to the park and paint for a while."

"Yes, you should do that while you still have good sunlight left. And feel free to take my car, since I won't need it anymore today. That rental car of yours is too small," Orin said, already pulling off his tie as he headed up the stairs.

She could tell he was somewhat upset about how the luncheon had gone. Evidently, he had assumed, or had been led to believe, that winning the Senate seat would be a piece of cake. It probably would have been if Reggie Westmoreland hadn't decided to throw his hat into the ring at the eleventh hour.

And she had to admit that although her father's

speech had been good, Reggie's speech had been better. Instead of making generalities, he had hammered down specifics, and he had delivered the speech eloquently. And it had seemed that as his gaze moved around the room while he was speaking, his eyes would seek her out. Each time they'd done so and she'd gazed into them, she'd felt she could actually see barely concealed desire in their dark depths. She had sat there with the hardened nipples of her breasts pressed tightly against her blouse the entire time.

And all she'd had to do was to study his lips to recall how those same lips had left marks all over her body, how they, along with his tongue, had moved over these same breasts, licking, sucking and nibbling on them.

After the luncheon was over, instead of dallying about, she had rushed her father out, needing to leave to avoid any attempts Reggie might have made to approach her again. She would not have been able to handle it if he had done so, and it would only have raised Senator Reed's suspicions. For some reason, the older man was making her every move his business.

Olivia had changed clothes and was gathering her art bag to sling over her shoulders when her cell phone rang. Not recognizing the local number, she answered the call.

"Hello?"

"Meet me someplace."

She got weak in the knees at the sound of the deep, husky voice. She really didn't have to ask, but she did so anyway. "Who is this?"

"This is Reggie Westmoreland, Wonder Woman."

Olivia pulled into the parking lot of Chase's Place, wondering for the umpteenth time how she had let Reggie Westmoreland talk her into meeting him there. The restaurant, he'd said, was closed on Mondays, but since he knew the owner, there would not be a problem with them meeting there for privacy.

When she'd indicated she did not want to be seen meeting with him, he'd told her to park in the rear of the building. She hated the idea of everything being so secretive, but she knew it was for the best.

Of all the never-in-a-million-years coincidences, why did she have to have an affair—one night or otherwise—with the one man her father could not stand at the moment?

Doing as Reggie had advised, she drove around to the rear and parked beside a very nice silver-gray Mercedes, the same one she'd seen Reggie driving Saturday night. After getting out and checking her watch for the time, she walked up to the back door of the restaurant and knocked. It opened immediately. A man who was almost as tall as Reggie and just as handsome opened the door and smiled at her before stepping aside to let her in.

"Olivia?" he asked, continuing to smile, as he closed the door behind her.

She was so busy studying his face, noting the similarities between him and Reggie, that she almost jumped when he uttered her name. Like Reggie, he was extremely handsome, but she didn't miss the gold band on his finger. "Yes?" she said finally.

"I'm Chase Westmoreland," he said, extending his hand. "Reggie is already here and is in one of the smaller offices, waiting for you. I'll take you to him."

"Thanks." And then, because curiosity got the best of her, she asked, "Are you one of Reggie's brothers?"

The man's chuckle floated through the air as he led her down a hallway. "No, Reggie has five brothers, but I'm not one of them. I'm his cousin."

"Oh. The two of you favor one another," she pointed out.

"Yes, all we Westmorelands look alike."

After walking down a long hallway, they stopped in front of a closed door. "Reggie is in here," Chase said, grinning. "It was nice meeting you."

Olivia smiled. "And it was nice meeting you as well, Chase." And then he was gone. She turned toward the closed door and took a deep breath before turning the handle.

Reggie stood the moment he heard voices on the other side of the door. This was the only place he could think of where he and Olivia could meet without fear of a reporter of some sort invading their privacy. The political campaign had begun officially today, and already all the sides were trying to dig up something on the others.

He'd told Brent that he wanted a campaign that focused strictly on the issues. He wasn't into dirty political games. He felt the voters should get to know the candidates, learn their stance on the issues and then decide which offered more of what they were looking for. If they wanted something different, then he was their man, and if they were used to the do-nothing agenda that Reed had implemented over the past four years, then they needed to go with Jeffries, since it was a sure bet that he was Reed's clone.

As soon as the door opened, his heart began hammering wildly in his chest, and the moment Olivia walked into the room and their gazes met, it took everything he possessed not to cross the floor and pull her into his arms and taste those lips he'd enjoyed so much a couple of nights ago.

Instead of coming farther into the room, she closed the door behind her and then leaned back on it, watching him. Waiting. His hands balled into fists at his sides. He smiled and said, "Wonder Woman." It wasn't a question; it was a statement. He knew who she was.

The butterflies in Olivia's stomach intensified

as they flew off in every direction. As she looked across the room at the extremely handsome man, she couldn't help but pose the one question that had been on her mind since they'd met earlier, at the luncheon. "How did you recognize me?" she asked in a soft-spoken voice.

He smiled, and she actually felt her heart stop. She felt her body begin to get hot all over. "Your lips gave you away. I recognized them. I would know your lips anywhere," he said. His voice was deep and throaty.

Olivia frowned, finding that strange. But it must have made some sense, at least to him, because he *had* been able to recognize her.

"What about you? You recognized me also. How?" he asked.

"I'm an artist, at least I am in my spare time. I study faces. I analyze every symmetrical detail. Although you were wearing a mask, and I couldn't see the upper part of your face, I zeroed in on the parts I could see." She decided not to tell him that there was more to it than his face. It had been his height that had first drawn her attention, and the way he'd tilted his head and his broad shoulders. If she could find the words to describe him, they would be, in addition to handsome—tall, dark…Westmoreland.

"I guess both of us can see things others might miss," he said.

"Yes, I guess we can," she agreed.

The room got silent, and she could feel it. That same sexual chemistry that had overtaken them that night, that had destroyed their senses to the point where they hadn't wanted to do anything else but go somewhere and be alone together, was still potent.

"Please come join me. I promise not to bite."

His words broke into her thoughts, and she couldn't help but smile. It was on the tip of her tongue to say, yes, he did bite and that she'd had numerous passion marks on her body to prove it. However, she had a feeling from the glint in his eyes that he'd realized the slipup the moment she had. His eyes darkened, and she felt heat settling everywhere his gaze touched.

She breathed in a deep breath before moving away from the door. She glanced around. The room was apparently a little game room. It had a love seat, a card table, a refrigerator and a television.

"This is where my cousins and brothers get together to play cards on occasion," said Reggie, breaking into her thoughts. "They used to rotate at each other's homes, but after they married and started having kids, they couldn't express themselves like they wanted whenever they were losing. So we decided to find someplace to go where we could be as loud and as colorful as we wanted to be."

She nodded and remembered how things were when her brothers used to have their friends over for poker. Some of their choice words would burn her ears. She then crossed the room to sit on the love seat.

He remained standing and was staring at her, making her feel uncomfortable. She cleared her throat. "You wanted to meet with me," she said, reminding him of why they were there.

He smiled. "Yes, and do you know why?"

"Yes," she said, holding his gaze. "It wouldn't take much to figure out that now that you know my father is one of the men you'll be running against in a few months, you want to establish an understanding between us. You want us to pretend that Saturday night never happened and that we've never met."

He continued to stare at her intently. "Is that what you think?"

She blinked. "Yes, of course. Under these circumstances, there's no way we can be seen together or even let anyone in on the fact that we know each other."

"I don't see why not. I'm running against your father, not you, so it shouldn't matter," he said.

Olivia felt her heart pounding hard in her chest. "But it does matter. Orin Jeffries is my father, and he and his campaign staff consider you the enemy," she said truthfully, although she hadn't meant to do so.

Reggie shook his head. "It's unfortunate they feel that way. I'm not his enemy. I'm his opponent in a Senate race. It's nothing personal, and I was hoping no one would make it such."

Olivia didn't know what to say. She knew Senator Reed, who seemed to be calling the shots as to how her father ran his campaign, could be ruthless at times. She had overheard the whispered conversations that took place at her table during lunch. She knew that the man had no intentions of letting this be a clean campaign, and that bothered her because it was so unlike her father to get involved in something so manipulative and underhanded.

"I'm sorry, but it will be personal. I don't agree, but politics is politics," she heard herself saying, knowing it wasn't an acceptable excuse. "If I became involved with you in any way, it would be equal to treason in my father's eyes. Things are too complicated."

"Only if we let them be. I still say us meeting and going out on occasion don't involve your father, just me and you."

She shook her head as she stood. It was time to go. She really should not have come. "I need to go."

"But you just got here," he said softly in that sexy voice that did things to her nervous system.

"I know, but coming here was a mistake," she said.

"Then why did you?" he asked softly.

She met his gaze and knew she would tell him the truth. "I felt that I should. Saturday night was a first of its kind for me. I've never left a party with someone I truly didn't know, and I've never had a one-night stand. But I did with you because I felt the chemistry. One of the reasons I came today was that I needed to see if the chemistry between us was real or a figment of my imagination."

"And what's your verdict?" he asked, holding her gaze.

She didn't hesitate in responding. "It's real."

"Does that frighten you?"

"It does not so much frighten me as confuse me. Like I said, I've never responded to a man this way before."

"And what was the other reason you came tonight?"

"We never took our masks off, and I needed to know how you were able to recognize me today. I got the answers to both of my questions, so I should leave now."

"But what about me? Aren't you interested in knowing why I wanted to see you again? Why I asked for us to meet?" He was staring intently at her, and his gaze seemed to touch her all over.

"Why did you want to see me?" she asked.

He slowly moved across the room to stand in front of her, and her pulse began beating rapidly, and heat began to settle between her thighs from his closeness. "Your lips were one reason."

"My lips?" she asked, raising a brow. He seemed to be searching her face, but she could tell his main focus was her lips.

"I claimed them as mine that night," he said in a husky whisper. "I just needed to know if they still are."

And before she could catch her next breath, he pulled her into his arms and captured her mouth with his.

They were still his.

This was what he needed to know. This was the very reason he had kept breathing since Saturday, Reggie thought as he hungrily mated with Olivia's mouth. The memories that had consumed him over the past forty-eight hours had nothing on the real thing. And she was responding to his kiss, feasting on his mouth as greedily as he was feasting on hers. Their masks were gone but not their passion.

He hadn't expected the fires to ignite so quickly, but already they were practically burning out of control. Her body was pressed fully against his, and he could feel every heated inch of her, just like he was certain she could feel every inch of him. Hard. Aroused. He knew he needed to pull back from her mouth to take a much-needed breath, but he couldn't. He had thought of kissing her, dreamed of kissing her, every since the morning they'd parted. His tongue was tangling with hers, and it seemed he couldn't get enough.

Instantly, he knew the moment she began withdrawing, and he pulled back, but not before tracing the outline of her lips with the tip of his tongue while tamping down on the stimulating effect the kiss had had on him.

"I really do need to leave." Her words lacked conviction, and he couldn't help but notice that she had wrapped her arms around his neck and hadn't yet released him. He also took note that her mouth was mere inches from his, and she hadn't pulled back.

Making a quick decision for both of them, he said, "Please stay and let's talk. Will you stay a while longer if I promise not to kiss you again? There's so much I want to know about you. I won't ask you anything about your father and his campaign, just about you."

"What good would it do, Reggie?" she asked, saying his name for the first time. The sound of it off her lips produced flutters in the pit of his stomach.

"I think it will appease our curiosity and maybe help us make some sense as to why we became attracted to each other so quickly and so deeply," he responded. "Why the chemistry between us is so strong."

Olivia pulled her arms from around his neck, thinking that what he was suggesting wasn't a good idea, but neither was kissing. But then she really didn't want to leave, and she had to admit that she'd wondered why they had hit it off so quickly and easily. But it didn't take a rocket scientist to figure out some of the reasons. He was an extremely handsome man, something she had recognized even with the mask. And his approach that night had not been egotistical or arrogant. She had somehow known he was someone she could have fun with and whose company she could enjoy.

And those things had been verified in the most intimate way.

"And we'll just talk?" she asked, making sure they understood each other.

"Yes, and about no one but us. That way you can't feel disloyal to your father."

She inhaled deeply. "But I still do," she admitted openly.

He didn't say anything for a moment. "Let me ask you something." At her nod, he asked, "If we would have met at any other time and if I was not your father's political opponent, would he have a problem with you dating me?"

She knew the answer to that, since her father had never been the kind of dad who cross-examined his children's dates. He had always accepted her judgment in that area. Now, her brothers had been another matter, especially Duan. "No, I think he wouldn't have a problem with it," she said truthfully.

"That's good to know, and that's why we should move forward on the premise that the campaign should not affect our relationship." His voice and smile conveyed that he truly believed what he was saying.

"But how can it not?" she asked, wishing things were that simple.

"Because we won't let it," he responded. "First of all, we need to acknowledge that we are in a relationship, Olivia."

She shook her head. "I can't do that, because we really don't have a relationship. We just slept together that night."

"No, it was more than that. It might have been a one-night stand, but I never intended *not* to find you after you left the Saxon on Sunday morning. In fact, I took this to a jewelry store this morning to see if I could trace where it was originally purchased," he said, pulling her diamond earring from his pocket. "It might have taken me a while, but eventually, I would have found you, even if I had to tear this town up doing so," he said, handing the earring to her.

She took it and studied it, remembering just when she had purchased the pair. It had been when she'd gotten her first position at the Louvre Museum. These diamonds had cost more than the amount of her first paycheck. But it had been a way for her to celebrate.

"Thank you for returning it." She slipped the earring into her pants pocket and then looked back at him. "So, what do you want to talk about?"

"I want to know everything about you. Over dinner. In here. Just the two of us."

She licked her lips and noticed immediately how his gaze had been drawn to the gesture. "And you promise no kissing, right?"

He chuckled. "Not unless you initiate it. If you do, then I won't turn you down."

She couldn't help but smile at that. "You mentioned dinner, but the restaurant isn't open today."

"No, it isn't, but Chase will make an exception for us. Will you join me here for dinner so we can talk and get to know each other?"

She was very much aware that if her father knew she was here, spending time with Reggie, he would think she was being disloyal, but she knew she truly wasn't. If at any time Reggie shifted the conversation to her father, as if pumping her for information about him, she would leave. But for now, she owed it to herself to do something that made her happy for a change, as long as she was not hurting anyone. If Duan or Terrence had been caught up in a similar situation, there was no way her father would have asked them to stop seeing that person. She should not be made the exception.

Olivia knew Reggie was waiting for her answer. "And our time here together will be kept confidential?"

He smiled. "Yes. Like I said, this is about you

and me, and not the campaign. As far as I'm concerned, one has nothing to do with the other."

"Then, yes, I'll join you here for dinner," she said after taking a long, deep breath.

Six

"I know your favorite color is lavender, but tell me something else about Olivia Jeffries, and before you ask, I want to know everything," Reggie said as he sat in the chair at the table while Olivia sat across from him, on the love seat, with her feet curled beneath her. They were both sipping wine and trying to rekindle that comfort zone between them.

Chase had been kind enough to take their food order and had indicated that he would be serving dinner to them shortly. He had given them a bottle of wine, two wineglasses, a tablecloth and eating utensils. Together, the two of them had set the table.

Reggie wondered if being here with him reminded her of how intimate things had been between them on Saturday night. They had shared dinner then, but only after spending hours making love, to the point where they were famished.

"I'm the baby in the family," she said, smiling. "I have two older brothers."

"And I know the Holy Terror is one of them," Reggie said, grinning. "He went to school with a couple of my cousins and two of my brothers. In fact, my brother Quade was on his football team in high school. I understand the Holy Terror has mellowed over the years."

Olivia chuckled. "It depends on what you mean by 'mellowed.' Both of my brothers tend to be overprotective at times, but Duan is worse than Terrence, since he's the oldest. Duan is thirty-six, and Terrence is thirty-four."

"And you are?" he asked, knowing a lot of women didn't like sharing their age.

"I'm twenty-seven. What about you?"

"Thirty-two."

Reggie took a sip of his wine and then asked, "Is Duan the one you sent the text message to on Saturday night?"

"Are you kidding?" she said, chuckling. "Duan would have been on the first flight back home, and he would not have erased your number. He would have had you thoroughly checked out. He has a lot of friends in law enforcement. He used to be a police detective. Now he owns a private investigation company. I sent the text message to Terrence. I can handle him a lot easier than I can Duan."

Reggie nodded. "So why is a beautiful girl like you living so far away from home, in Paris?"

She smiled. "Working. I've always wanted to work at the Louvre Museum in Paris, and I was hired right out of grad school as a tour guide. I had to start at the bottom, but I didn't mind if that's what it would take to work my way up the ladder to be an art curator. It took me almost four years, but I finally made it. I've been a curator for almost a year."

"Congratulations," he said and meant it.

"Thanks."

"So do you plan to make Paris your permanent home?" he asked, watching her sip her wine. He liked the way her lips curved around her glass. He had noticed this detail about her on Saturday night, and it had been a total turn-on…just like it was now.

"I love living over there. I miss being home sometimes, but I've managed to return for the holidays. My brothers and I make it a point to be home for Christmas. But my dream is to return home in a few years, when I've saved up enough money to establish an art gallery." She smiled wistfully.

He nodded. "So over the years, you've come home only during the holidays?"

"Yes."

He wondered if that had anything to do with the fact that her mother had walked out on them a couple of days before Christmas, according to Brent. Reggie could only imagine how disruptive that particular Christmas had to have been for them. "And how long do you plan to stay this time?"

She didn't say anything at first, just stared into her wineglass for a while. Finally, she said, "Until the election is over."

She glanced up and met his gaze, and he breathed in deeply and said, "We won't let that matter now, remember?" he reminded her gently.

"Yes," she said softly. "I remember." She shifted positions in her seat. "So, now, tell me about Reggie Westmoreland."

He took another sip of his wine and then leaned forward in his chair, resting his arms on his thighs. "I'm the youngest son of my parents. Multiple births run in my family. My father is a fraternal twin. My uncle John and my aunt Evelyn have five sons and one daughter."

"Chase is one of their sons?" she interrupted.

He smiled. "Yes, and Chase is a twin. His twin, Storm, is a fireman. So in their birth order, my cousins are Dare, who is the sheriff of College Park, Thorn, who races and builds motorcycles, Stone, who is a writer and writes adventure novels as Rock Mason, the twins Chase and Storm, and

Delaney, the only girl. Delaney and I are the same age and are very close."

"I've heard about Thorn, and, of course, I've read a few Rock Mason novels. And I remember reading years ago about your cousin Delaney and how she married a sheikh. That's awesome."

"Yeah, we all think it is, although I have to say, her brothers weren't too happy about it at first, especially with her leaving the country to live in the Middle East. But her husband, Jamal, is a real nice guy, and everyone looks forward to her trips home. All my cousins are married with children."

"What about your siblings? I understand there are quite a few. Are there twins on your side, too?" she asked.

"Yes. My oldest brother is Jared, and he is a divorce attorney here in the city. Spencer lives in California and is the financial adviser in the family. Durango lives in Montana and is a park ranger. He's thinking about retiring to play a bigger role in his horse-breeding business. And then there are the twins—Ian and Quade. Ian owns a resort on Lake Tahoe, and Quade used to work for the government, but now he owns a number of security firms around the country. Quade and his wife are the parents of triplets, and they live in Carolina, although they have another home in Jamaica."

"Wow! You weren't kidding when you said

multiple births run in your family. Are your brothers married?"

"Yes, and happily so. I'm the only single Westmoreland living in Atlanta. My father has a brother, Uncle Corey, who lives in Montana. He also has triplets, Casey, Clint and Cole, and they are all married."

At that moment, there was a knock on the door, and seconds later Chase entered with their food. "Everything smells delicious," Olivia said, getting to her feet to help place the plates on the table.

Chase smiled. "I hope the two of you enjoy it," he said, then left them alone again.

Once they were seated at the table, Reggie glanced over at her and smiled. "I'm glad you decided to stay."

Olivia returned his smile.

During dinner Olivia was so tuned in to Reggie that she could only stare at him and listen to everything he was saying. He told her about the other family of Westmorelands, the ones living in Colorado, whom his father had discovered when he decided to research the family history a year ago. A family reunion was being held later this month in Texas, where both the Atlanta-based Westmorelands and the Denver-based Westmorelands would be getting together and officially meeting for the first time. It sounded exciting, especially to someone whose family was limited to two brothers and a father. Both of her sets of grandparents were deceased, and both of her parents had been only children.

"Would you like some more dessert?" he asked.

Reggie's question reclaimed her thoughts, and she smiled over at him. He had kept his word, and although the attraction they shared was there, flowing blatantly between them, they had been able to harness it while sharing information about each other. A part of Olivia wasn't sure why they had decided to spend time together when nothing would ever come of it, but they had. Once again, the desire to be together, if only to breathe the same air and share conversation, had driven them to defy what others around them felt they should do.

"No, thanks. I do have to leave. I told my father I was going to the park to paint."

"I'm glad you agreed to meet with me and I'm sorry if I placed you in an awkward position."

"You didn't," she said. "I mentioned to Dad that I was going to the park before you called. I just didn't tell him of my change of plans, because he was resting."

"Would you have done otherwise?" he asked her.

She knew she would be honest and said, "No, he would have forbidden it. And that's the reason why, as much as I enjoyed sharing dinner and conversation with you, Reggie, we can't do it again. I hope you understand."

He met her eyes. "No, I don't understand, because like I said earlier, Olivia, the campaign doesn't concern our relationship."

"The press won't see it that way, and they would have a field day with the story of you and I being involved. I refuse to sneak around to see you." She stood. "I need to go."

Reggie stood as well. He knew he couldn't detain her any longer, but he was more determined than ever to see her again and spend time with her. And he didn't want them to sneak around, either. There had to be a way, and he was determined to find it. "I enjoyed our time together, Olivia."

She held out her hand to him. "So did I. Thank you."

Reggie took the hand she offered, felt the heat the moment he touched it and knew she felt the heat as well. His fingers tightened on hers, and they both were aware of the sensations flowing between them. This wasn't the first time such a thing had happened. It always did when they came in contact with each other.

It was she who tugged her hand away first. "And thanks again for returning my earring."

"You're welcome."

And then Olivia turned and moved toward the door. Before she opened it, she glanced back over her shoulder, saw his unwavering stare, deciphered the intense desire in his eyes. She still felt the heat of his touch on her hand.

She wanted to go back to him, wrap her arms around his neck, but she knew she could not. She would not regret the time she'd spent with him on Saturday night or today. But she was realistic enough to know that as long as Reggie Westmoreland was her father's opponent in the Senate race, her father would never accept her dating a Westmoreland. So from this day forward, she would have fond memories of their times together, but they would have to sustain her throughout the campaign and later, when she returned to Paris.

"Olivia?"

She had already opened the door to leave when she heard him call her name. Swallowing deeply, she stopped and turned around. "Yes?"

"No matter what, you will forever be my Wonder Woman."

She felt the tightness in her throat and fought the tears that had begun clouding her eyes. *And you, Reggie Westmoreland, will forever be the man that I wished I'd had the opportunity to get to know better,* she thought.

Their gazes held for the longest time, and then she turned and walked out the door and closed it behind her.

* * *

Olivia was surprised to find her father had already gone to bed by the time she returned home. At some point, he had come downstairs and fixed a pot of vegetable soup, which he'd left warming on the stove for her. A part of her felt awful about her deceit. She'd been served a delicious full-course meal at Chase's Place, while her father had been home, eating alone.

She quickly realized that he'd not eaten alone when she noticed two of everything in the sink and the lipstick on the rim of one of the coffee cups. She smiled. The lipstick was the shade Cathy usually wore, which meant there was a good possibility that her father's secretary had joined him for dinner.

She went upstairs and was about to undress for her shower when her cell phone rang. "Hello."

"Hey, Libby, I heard you were home."

"Duan! Where are you? How have you been?"

She heard her brother's deep laugh. "Still asking a thousand questions, are you? I've been fine. How are things there?"

"Umm, so-so. Dad gave his first speech today, and I thought it was great, but he feels his opponent did better."

"Well, did his opponent do better, Libby?"

His question threw her. Why would Duan ask her something like that? "Let's just say that they both did well, but Westmoreland made a direct hit on all the issues, whereas Dad just skated across the surface, like Senator Reed used to do."

"Politics as usual," Duan said. "I told Dad that I don't know squat about politics, but I'd think the people would want some fresh and innovative ideas. With Senator Reed tagging along, there's no way Dad can represent change."

Olivia nodded. She was glad she wasn't the only person in the family who thought that.

Duan went on. "And it's a shame that he's running against Reggie Westmoreland. I heard he's a nice guy. His cousin Dare is the sheriff of College Park. I've worked with Dare before, and I like him. Most of the Westmorelands that I know are good people."

"Dad thinks he's the enemy," Olivia said.

"I'm sorry that Dad feels that way. I was hoping this would be a clean campaign. I bet it's Senator Reed who's trying to make it dirty."

She could hear the dislike in her brother's voice. "So you will make it home for the barbecue next Saturday?" she asked him. In two weeks there would be a massive outdoor cookout in Atlanta-Fulton County Stadium for people to come out and meet all the candidates. Their father had asked her and her brothers to be there for the event so that the Jeffries family could show a united front.

"Yes, I'm in Detroit, but I hope to have everything wrapped up by then."

"Good." She looked forward to seeing both of her brothers. "Be safe, Duan."

"I will."

After leaving Chase's Place, Reggie decided to stop by and visit with his parents. He'd always admired his parents and the strength of their marriage. Everyone in the family knew the story of how James and Sarah Westmoreland had met and how it had been love at first sight. He couldn't help but chuckle when he thought about it now.

His mother and his aunt Evelyn had been the best of friends since childhood and had both been born and raised in Birmingham, Alabama. After graduating from high school, Evelyn had come to Atlanta to visit her aunt for the summer. During her first week in the city, she'd gone on a church picnic and met John Westmoreland. It had been love at first sight, and deciding not to waste any time, John and Evelyn had eloped the following week.

Evelyn had called Sarah to tell her the news, and being the levelheaded person that his mother was, Sarah could not believe or accept that someone could meet and fall in love at first glance. So Sarah had gone to Atlanta to talk some sense into Evelyn, only to meet John's twin brother, James, and fall in love with him at first sight as well. Two weeks later Sarah and James had married.

That had been nearly forty years ago, and his

parents' marriage was still going strong. There had been his mom's cancer scare a few years back, when she'd been diagnosed with breast cancer. But thankfully, she was now doing fine, although she made sure never to miss her annual checkups. His mother was a strong and determined woman who had the love and admiration of her family.

Although Reggie knew it was his mother's desire to see her last son happily wedded, he was in no hurry. He had a good career as an accountant, with a very prestigious client list, and in a couple of months, he would know if his future would include politics.

His thoughts then shifted to Olivia Jeffries. He had enjoyed the time they had spent together tonight. In bed or out, she was someone he liked being with, and it bothered him that she had refused to see him again because of her father. The last thing they needed was to let anyone or anything get in the way of what could be a promising relationship. He understood that she would be leaving the country to return to Paris once the election was over, but Saturday night and today had proven that they were good together. He had actually enjoyed sitting in the coziness of that room at Chase's Place with her while they did little more than engage in conversation with each other.

He had enjoyed studying her while she talked, watching her lips move with each and every word she enunciated. And she had been wearing the same perfume she'd had on Saturday night. It had been hard sitting there across from her, knowing that he had tasted every inch of her skin, had been inside her body and had brought her pleasure.

By the time he pulled into his parents' driveway, he knew there was no way he could willingly walk away from Olivia Jeffries. He didn't like the thought of the two of them sneaking around to see each other so her father wouldn't find out, but at the moment he didn't care. The bottom line was that he wanted to see her again and would do anything and everything in his power—even blackmail—to make it happen.

If Olivia thought she had seen or heard the last of him, she was sorely mistaken.

Seven

"I see you had a guest for dinner last night, Dad."

Olivia watched her father actually blush across the breakfast table and thought it was kind of cute that he seemed a little embarrassed.

"Ahh, yes, Cathy stopped by, and I invited her to stay for dinner."

"Oh, and why did she come by? Are the two of you working on another speech?"

"No, no," her father was quick to say. "She thought I wasn't in a good mood after yesterday's luncheon and wanted to cheer me up. She stopped by the bakery and brought me my favorite Danish. I thought that was kind of her."

"I think so, too, but then Cathy is a kind person. I like her."

Her father lifted a brow. "Do you really?"

Olivia looked over at him. She could tell her response was important to him. "Yes, and I always have. Over the years I thought she was not only a good secretary to you but a nice person, too. When I was younger and was dealing with a lot of girl stuff, I would often call Cathy."

Her father looked surprised. "You did?"

"Yes. Come on, Dad. You have to have known it was hard for me being the only girl in the house, and I couldn't talk to you, Duan and Terrence about *everything*."

"No, I guess not. I'm glad she was there for you then," her father said.

"Yes, and I'm glad she's here for you now, Dad."

Olivia watched as Orin's blush deepened. "Everything between me and Cathy is strictly business."

She was forced to hide her smile behind the rim of the coffee cup she'd brought to her lips. "Of course, Dad. I wasn't insinuating anything."

Half an hour later, after her father had left for work, Olivia decided to get dressed and go to the park and paint like she had planned to do the day before. She was about to head downstairs when her cell phone rang. For some reason, she knew who the caller was without looking. Her heart skipped several beats before she clicked the phone on. "Hello."

"Please meet with me again, Olivia."

She closed her eyes and breathed in deeply as the sensuous sound of his voice floated through her. "Reggie, I thought we decided that we wouldn't see each other again."

"I thought so, too, but I couldn't sleep last night. Thoughts of you kept invading my mind. I want to see you, Olivia. I want to be with you. Meet me today at noon. The Saxon Hotel. The same room number."

Her mind was suddenly flooded with memories of everything that had taken place in that room. And he wasn't the only one who'd been unable to sleep last night. Her body had been restless. Hot. She had dreamed of him several times, and at one point she had sat on the edge of the bed for what seemed like hours, recovering from the pleasurable memories that had swept through her, interrupting her night and filling her with a need she had never felt…until meeting Reggie.

"Will you come, Olivia? Please."

His voice was deep, quiet, yet persuasive. The sound of it poured over her skin like warm cream, and she couldn't fight it, because deep inside she wanted to be with him as much as he wanted to be with her.

She needed to see him again, to know, to understand and to explore the pull between them. Was it just sexual, or was it something else? Despite her decision not to become involved with him, she knew that she had to be with him at least one more time. These memories she was collecting would have to be enough to sustain her for the rest of her life.

"Yes," she said finally. "I'll meet you at noon."

Reggie paced the hotel room, glancing at his watch every so often. It was a few minutes before noon. He had had a news conference at nine but hadn't counted on a slew of reporters bombarding him after the news conference was over. Nor had he counted on the rumor that had quickly spread that his accounting firm, which employed over a hundred people, was facing possible bankruptcy and definite layoffs.

It was a lie that could easily be proven false, but not before mass pandemonium erupted at his business, and he'd spent part of the morning calming his employees' fears. He didn't have to think twice about where the lie had been generated, which made him angrier than hell. He'd never suspected that Orin Jeffries would allow his campaign staff to stoop so low.

For a moment he'd thought he would have to cancel this meeting with Olivia, but a part of him had refused to do it. She had consented to meet with him, and he would have moved heaven and hell to be here. Now he couldn't help wondering if she would show up. What if she had changed her mind? What if—

At that moment the door opened and Olivia walked in and his entire body went completely still. It seemed as if his heart picked that exact moment to stop beating. He was very much aware of how good she looked dressed in a pair of black tailored slacks and a light blue linen blouse.

She closed the door behind her and leaned against it, saying nothing but holding his gaze as intently as he was holding hers. He could now admit that although he had been drawn to her lips, the total package was what had captured his interest. She had the kind of presence that demanded attention, and just like at the Firemen's Masquerade Ball and yesterday, she was getting his again today. In droves.

In addition to checking her out, he was trying to get a read on her but couldn't. The sexual chemistry had hit the airwaves the moment she had walked through the door. With them, it couldn't be helped. But what about her attitude? he wondered. She had said yesterday that she didn't want them to become involved. Yet when he had defied her wishes and had called and asked her to meet with him here, she had accepted.

What was she expecting from him? What was he expecting from her?

He definitely knew what he wanted, but wanting and expecting were two different things. For the moment he was just glad to have her here, in this hotel room, alone with him. Had she come to spend time with him or to chew him out for having the audacity to call and ask her to meet with him? He was certain he was about to find out.

"Hello, Olivia."

"Reggie." And then, with her gaze still locked firmly with his, she moved away from the door and walked toward him.

His heart somehow began beating again, and it was only when she came to a stop directly in front of him that he allowed his gaze to shift and took note of the cut of her blouse. The low, square cut showed the nice swell of her breasts. They were breasts he had tasted before and was dying to taste again. Not surprisingly, something primal stirred inside him. His heart rate increased, and he breathed in deeply as a way to slow it down.

He cleared his throat. "I ordered lunch," he heard himself say and watched as she glanced behind him to see the table that had been set for two. "I'll call them to deliver the food when we're ready to eat," he said and drew a somewhat shaky breath.

She reached out and smoothed her hand along the back of his neck. "Are you hungry now, Reggie?" she asked, her voice an octave lower than he remembered.

He swallowed thickly. The feel of her fingers on his skin was pure torture. "It's up to you, since you're my guest."

A smile touched her lips at the corners. "In that case, we can wait. I'd rather do this now." And then she leaned up on tiptoe and connected her mouth to his.

At that moment whatever control he had been holding on to broke, and he instantly swept her into his arms without disconnecting their mouths. He wanted to head directly for the bedroom, but at that moment the only thing he could do was stand there with her in his arms and savor her this way, not sure when or if he would be granted the opportunity to do so again. He intended to make this their day, just like Saturday had been their night.

On the way to the hotel, Brent had tried to pin him down as to where he was going. He had told his friend that he was to be disturbed only if there was an emergency. He could tell Brent had wanted more information, but none had been forthcoming. What he did on his personal time was his business, and this lunch was on his personal time. And he was feasting on what he enjoyed most. Olivia's mouth.

He wasn't sure what had changed her mind since yesterday, when she had been adamant about not getting involved with him, but he was just glad she had. There was only so much a man could take.

He finally pulled back from her mouth. It was then that she nuzzled against his ear. The tip of her tongue trailed a path beneath it, and then she whispered. "I want to make love with you again—"

Before she could finish her words, he headed in the direction of the bedroom, sidestepping the table set for two. She laughed when he gently tossed her on the bed, then captured her laughter with his mouth when he quickly joined her there. And then it was back on. The heat was blazing. They didn't have a moment to waste, and they both knew it. As they lay fully clothed in bed, with their mouths joined in the most intimate way, their tongues dueled, tangled and mated. She refused to stay still. She was moving all over the place, and he eventually placed a thigh over hers. She had become wild, so bold and wanton. And he loved it.

She pulled her mouth back and met his gaze, their hearts pounding loudly in the room. "Make love to me, Reggie. Now," she said.

She didn't have to say the words twice. He moved off the bed and quickly undressed, trying not to rip the buttons off his shirt in his haste. And then, when he was completely naked, except for the condom he had taken the time to put on, he went for her, pulled her toward him to remove her blouse and bra before tackling her shoes, slacks and panties.

When he had pulled the latter two down her hips to reveal the lushness of her feminine mound, he knew he had to taste her right then. He tossed the items of clothing aside and held down her hips at the same time that his mouth lowered to her, kissing her intimately, with a hunger and greed that made her tremble and moan incoherently. But he didn't let up. His tongue was desperate to reacquaint itself with the taste it had relished on Saturday, and he intended to get his fill. And her body responded, generating the sweetness he wanted, and he mercilessly savored her.

He felt her hands lock around his head as if to hold his mouth in place, but that wasn't needed. He wasn't going anyplace until he got enough, and that wouldn't be anytime soon. He proved his point by plunging his tongue deeper inside of her, absorbing the wetness of her sensuality, which was being produced in abundance just for him.

Reggie finally pulled back and licked his lips, while his eyes traveled down her entire body, taking in every inch and every curve, the texture of her skin and the fullness of her breasts, which seemed to be begging for his mouth.

Leaning upward, he brushed his lips against a taut nipple, liking the sound of the quick breath that got caught in her throat. He proceeded to sample her nipples, finding both tantalizingly hot.

"Come inside me, please."

Olivia's tortured moan had Reggie moving his body over hers. When his heated shaft was at the opening of her feminine mound, he met her gaze, and then, with a hungry growl, he pushed deep inside of her.

Olivia closed her eyes as pleasure washed through her. What was there about being joined to Reggie that made her feel such joy, such mind-blowing pleasure and such spellbinding ecstasy? She felt him lift her legs, and she wrapped them around his waist while he thrust inside of her with whipcord speed and precision. Everything about him was affecting her in an elemental way, and she could barely stifle her moans as she was consumed by a tide of red-hot passion. It was only with him that she could feel not only taken but possessed. Only with him could she be not only driven but also contained. And he was making love to her without any restraint and with a voracious need, which was fueling her own. And every time the hard muscles of his stomach pressed against hers, pinning her beneath him, she trembled from the inside out.

And then an orgasm rammed through her. Never before had she felt anything so profound. She cried out his name. And he used his tongue, lips and mouth to absorb her cries of pleasure, her moans of passion. Instead of letting up, he pressed on and thrust deeper.

The flames ignited, flared and then burned in the very center of her, and when an explosion ripped through her a second time, he was there, and she felt his shaft expand before exploding in his release. And as passion tumbled her over into the depths of turbulent, sensual waters, she cried his name once more before she felt herself drowning in a sea of ecstasy.

Propped up on his elbow, Reggie stared down at Olivia. In the middle of the day, she had actually drifted off to sleep. He smiled, understanding why. He had shown her no mercy in taking them both through waves and waves of pure pleasure. Somewhere in the back of his mind, he heard the sound of his cell, but at that moment he chose to ignore it. His main focus, his total concentration, was on the most beautiful creature he had ever laid eyes on.

He glanced over at the clock on the nightstand. They had been in the room for two hours already— two hours of nonstop lovemaking in which he would get hard again before even coming out of her. They would start another bout of lovemaking right on the tail end of the previous one. Nothing like this had ever happened to him before. He felt totally obsessed with this woman.

He could vividly recall the first moment he had seen her at the Firemen's Masquerade Ball. He had known then, just like he knew now, that she was the one that he would make his. At the time he just hadn't known the depth to which he would do so. Now he did.

And he also understood why his brothers and cousins seemed so happy these days, so blissfully content. They had been able to find that one person who they knew was their soul mate. The question of the hour was, how was he going to convince Olivia that she was his? Especially considering the fact that they were sneaking around just to be together.

He wanted to introduce her to his family. He especially wanted her to get to know his mother and his brothers' and cousins' wives. He wanted to take her to the Westmoreland family reunion, which would be held in Texas at the end of the month. He wanted to take her to one of Thorn's motorcycle races later this year. There were so many things he wanted to share with her. But the most important thing of all was his life.

There was no need to tell her that he loved her, because she wouldn't understand that one thing about being a Westmoreland was recognizing your mate when you saw her or him. Although, he thought, with a smile, he would have to admit some of his cousins and brothers had refused to accept their fate at first. But in the end it hadn't done any good. Love had zapped their senses just the same. And it had done the same thing to him. It had hit him like a ton of bricks on Saturday night, and like his parents, he had fallen in love at first sight.

She had her defenses down now, but he wouldn't be surprised if they were back up before she left the hotel today. It didn't matter. He was not going to let her deny them what was rightfully theirs to have. She didn't know it yet, but in time she would. No matter what the situation was between him and her father regarding the campaign, it had no bearing on the two of them.

He noticed her eyes fluttering before they fully opened, and then she was staring up at him. She had to be hungry now. He would feed her, and then he would make love to her again.

Or so he thought. Suddenly she lifted her body and pushed him back onto the covers to straddle him, placing her knees on the sides of his hips to seemingly hold him immobile. She tilted her head back and looked down at him. And smiled. He felt the effects of that smile like a punch to his gut, and his shaft suddenly got hard, totally erect.

"I thought you would be hungry," he said, reaching out and placing the palm of his hand at the back of her neck.

"I am," she whispered, holding his eyes with her own. "For you."

He drew her head down to brush his lips against hers. "And I for you."

When he released her mouth, she glanced at him with a confused look in her eyes. "What are you doing to me, Reggie Westmoreland? How do you have the ability to make me feel wild and reckless? Make me want to yield to temptation?"

A hot rush of desire sent shivers through his

body. "I should be asking you the same thing, Olivia Jeffries."

And then she lowered herself on him, and he knew it was a good thing he'd already donned a new condom, because there was no way he could have said stop when she embedded him inside of herself to the hilt. The look on her face told him that she was proud of her accomplishment. She had wanted, so she had taken.

And then she began moving, slowly at first and then with a desperation that sent fire surging through his loins and made it feel as if the head of his shaft was about to explode. But she kept moving, dangling her twin globes in front of his face with every downward motion.

He reached out and grabbed hold of one, brought it to his mouth, and she threw her head back as she continued to ride him in a way he had never been ridden before. The woman had power in her thighs, in her hips and in her inner muscles, and she was using them to make shivers race all through him.

In retaliation, he covered her breasts with his kisses, using his lips and tongue to push her over the same edge that he was close to falling from. And when an explosion hit, he bucked until they were almost off the bed, but then her thighs nearly held him immobile. His body was locked so tightly with hers, he wondered if they would be able to separate when the time came. And at that moment he really didn't care if they couldn't. He would love to stay inside of her forever, in the place where he would one day plant his seed for their child.

That thought triggered another explosion inside of him, and he groped hard for sanity when Olivia came apart on top of him. Her inner muscles clamped him tightly, and she drew every single thing she could out of him. His lungs felt like they were about to collapse in his throat when he tried to keep from hollering out. Burying his face in her chest, he found a safe haven right between her breasts. He knew from this day forward that whatever it took, one day he would make her totally, completely and irrevocably his.

"We never ate lunch, did we?" Olivia asked as she slid back into her slacks.

"No, and I owe you an apology for that," Reggie said, pulling up his pants. He stopped what he was doing and stared at her, watched how she was struggling with the buttons on her blouse.

"Come here, Olivia."

She glanced over at him and smiled before crossing the room to him. "I don't know why I wore this thing when it has so many buttons. It's not like I didn't know that you would be taking it off me."

He didn't say anything as he took over buttoning her blouse. She was right. It did have a lot of buttons. That wouldn't have been so bad if his attention hadn't been drawn to her flesh-toned bra. "Your bra is my favorite color," he said, smiling down at her.

"I figured as much when I put it on," she said, grinning. "You were right. Flesh tone is a color."

"If you're hungry, we can still—"

"No. I noticed your cell phone went off a few times. You need to get back to work."

He chuckled. "Have you noticed the time, Olivia? The day is practically over. We've been here for five hours. It's past five o'clock." And he really wasn't bothered by it. "There. All done," he said, dropping his hands to his sides before he was tempted to do something, like pull her into his arms and kiss her.

"Thanks. Now I definitely need to know something," she said, looking up at him.

"What?"

"Do you have stock in this place?"

Another smile touched his lips. "Wish I did, but no."

"Then what kind of connections do you have?" she asked, with an expression on her face that said she was determined to know.

"My connection is my brother Quade. Dominic Saxon is his brother-in-law. Both recently became fathers. Quade has triplets—a son and two daughters and Dominic's wife, Taylor, gave birth to a son a few months ago."

"Oh. Proud fathers, I gather."

Reggie smiled. "Yes, they are."

He slipped into his shirt while he watched her stand before the dresser's mirror to redo her makeup. Although he knew he would probably get some resistance, he decided to go ahead and have his say. "I got the room again for this Saturday night, Olivia."

Olivia met his gaze in the mirror before slowly turning around to stare at him. He had just issued an open invitation, and it was one he wanted her to accept. She continued to stare into his dark eyes, and then she shifted her gaze to study his face. There was something, something she couldn't decipher, in his eyes and on his face.

"Coming here today was risky, Reggie," she finally said softly.

"I know," was his response. "But I had to see you."

"And I had to be with you," she said honestly.

Too late she wondered why she would admit such a thing to him, but deep down she knew the reason. She wanted him to know that she had wanted to be here and that she thought their time together was special.

Reggie crossed the room to her, and without giving him the chance to make the first move, she reached up and drew his mouth down to hers. And he kissed her with a gentleness that he had to fight to maintain.

When she released his mouth, he gazed down at her. "Sure you had enough?"

She licked her lips. "For now." She then smiled. "I'll get the rest on Saturday."

He lifted a hopeful brow. "You will come?"

She smiled. "Yes, I will come."

Although he knew they needed to finish getting dressed and be on their way, he reached out, caught her around the waist and pulled her gently into his arms, immediately reveling in the way her body seemed to cling to his, perfectly and in sync. And then he lowered his mouth to hers for a kiss that would keep him going strong until Saturday night, when they would come together once again.

Eight

"Cathy will be calling you later today, Libby."

Olivia lifted her gaze from her cereal bowl to glance over at her father, with a questioning look on her face. "For what reason?"

"To schedule all those fund-raisers that you and I will need to attend over the next couple of weeks, beginning this Saturday."

Panic shot through Olivia. "Not this Saturday night, I hope."

Her father quirked a thick brow. "No, it's Saturday midday at the home of Darwin Walker and his wife."

She nodded. Darwin and Terrence used to play

together for the Miami Dolphins. Last year Darwin, who, like Terrence, had retired from the NFL, moved to Atlanta after accepting a coaching position with the Falcons.

"And why are you concerned about Saturday night? Do you have plans or something?" Orin asked.

Olivia swallowed. She hated lying to her father, but there was no way she could tell him the truth. Running for political office had made him somewhat unreasonable, especially when it came to Reggie. She was convinced that the only reason he didn't like Reggie was that he was the main person standing in the way of him becoming a senator. However, she intended to do as Reggie had suggested and believe that the election had no bearing on what was developing between them.

She met her father's gaze. "Yes, I have plans. I ran into a friend at the party Saturday night, and we're getting together again this weekend." At least what she'd said wasn't a total lie.

Her father's features softened. "That's good. I've been feeling badly about asking you to put your life in Paris on hold to come here and be my escort for all these campaign events. I'm glad you've managed to squeeze in some fun time."

If only you knew just how much fun I've had thanks to Reggie, she thought.

Both she and her father resumed eating, and the

kitchen became quiet. There was something she needed to ask him, something she truly needed to know. The issue had been bothering her since she'd heard about it yesterday.

She glanced across the table at her father. He had resumed reading the paper and was flipping through the pages. She hated interrupting, but she had to. "Dad, can I ask you something?"

"Sure, sweetheart," Orin said, looking up to meet her gaze and placing the newspaper aside. "What is it?"

"Reggie Westmoreland," she said and watched her father's jaw flex.

"What about him, Libby?"

"Did you authorize any of your staff members to put out that false statement about his company facing bankruptcy and layoffs?"

Her father frowned. "Of course not. Why would I or my staff do something like that?"

"To discredit him."

His features tightened. "And you believe I would do something like that or give my staff permission to do so?"

"I don't want to believe that, but I'm not naive. I know how dirty politics can be, Dad."

Orin leaned back in his chair. "Are you taking up for Reggie Westmoreland?" he asked, studying her features.

She sighed deeply. "No, Dad, I'm not taking up

for anyone. Such tactics can backfire, so my concern is actually for you."

What she didn't say was that she was sure Reggie was aware of the rumor, which had circulated yesterday, but he hadn't mentioned it to her. Although he had to have been upset about it, Reggie had given her his full concentration and had kept his word not to mix his competition with her father and his relationship with her.

Now it was her turn to study her father's features, and she could see that what she'd said had him thinking. Was he so disjointed from his campaign staff that he truly didn't know what was going on? Did he not know what they were capable of?

"I'm having a meeting with my campaign staff this morning, and if I discover that someone on my staff is connected to yesterday's story in any way, they will be dismissed."

She came close to asking if that included Senator Reed. She had a feeling he was behind the rumor. "Thanks, Dad. I think it will be in your best interest in the long run."

"Where were you yesterday, Reggie? I tried reaching you all afternoon," Brent said, looking across the breakfast table at his friend. They were sitting in Chase's Place, where they had met for breakfast.

Reggie shrugged. "I was busy. Did anything come up that you couldn't handle?"

"Of course not." Brent set his coffee cup down, and his blue eyes studied Reggie intently. "But it would have been nice if I'd been able to contact you. Someone from *Newsweek* called to do an article on you. We're not talking about a local magazine, Reg. We're talking about *Newsweek*. You know how long I've been trying to get you national coverage."

Yes, Reggie did know, and he felt badly about it. But at the time all he could think about was that he wanted to spend uninterrupted time with Olivia. "I'm sorry about that, Brent."

"You're seeing her, aren't you?"

Reggie lifted a brow and met Brent's stare. "It depends on who you're referring to."

"Orin Jeffries's daughter."

Reggie leaned back in his chair. He and Brent had been friends for a long time, since grade school, actually. After attending college at Yale, Brent had worked for a number of years in Boston before moving back to Atlanta a few years ago to care for his elderly parents. A couple of months ago, Reggie had been the best man at Brent's wedding.

As far as Reggie was concerned, other than his brothers and cousins, there wasn't a man he trusted more. He met his best friend's eyes. "Yes, I'm seeing her."

Brent let out a deep sigh. "Do you think that's smart?"

Reggie chuckled. "Considering the fact that I plan to marry her sometime after the election, yes, I would have to say it's smart."

Brent's jaw dropped. "Marry!" And then he quickly glanced around, hoping no one had heard his outburst. After turning back around, he nervously brushed back a strand of blond hair that had fallen onto his face. "Reggie, you just met the woman on Monday at that luncheon."

"No," Reggie said, smiling, as he absently swirled the coffee around in his cup. "Actually, we met before then."

Brent lifted a brow. "When?"

"Saturday night, at the Firemen's Masquerade Ball."

"Saturday night?"

"Yes," replied Reggie.

"That wasn't even a week ago. Are you telling me you decided once you saw her at a party that you were going to marry her?"

"Something like that. And at the time I didn't know who she was. I found out her true identity on Monday, at that luncheon, the same time she found out mine." Reggie could only smile. Brent was staring at him like he had totally lost his mind. "Trust me, my friend, I haven't lost my mind. Just my heart."

Brent took a sip of his orange juice. His expression implied that he wished the juice was laced with vodka. "Do the two of you understand the implications of what you're doing? Hello," he said, putting emphasis on that single word. "Her father is your opponent in a Senate race."

"We're aware of that. However, we've decided that has nothing to do with what's going on between us," Reggie said.

"And you love her?" Brent asked incredulously.

"With all my heart and then some," Reggie answered truthfully.

He had thought about it a lot last night. To be honest, he hadn't been able to think about anything else. As crazy as it might seem to some people, yes, he had fallen in love with her. He had never been totally against marriage, especially since his family over the past seven years—starting with Delaney—seemed to be falling like flies into matrimony. He just knew he wouldn't ever settle down until the right woman came along. Because of his career and his decision to get into politics, he hadn't expected that to happen anytime soon. He thought he would at least be in his late thirties when he tied the knot, although he knew his mother wished otherwise.

"And she feels the same way?"

Brent's question invaded Reggie's thoughts. "Not sure. I've never asked her. In fact, I haven't even shared my feelings with her yet. It will be best to wait until after the campaign."

Brent took another gulp of his orange juice. "I swear, Reggie, you're going to give me heart failure."

Reggie smiled. "Don't mean to. I'm sure you remember when you met Melody. What did you tell me? You claimed you had fallen in love with her instantly."

"I did. But her father wasn't my political opponent," Brent countered.

"Shouldn't matter, and we intend not to let it affect our relationship, either. So wish us luck."

Brent couldn't help but smile. "Hey, man, what you need are prayers, and I'll be the first to send one up for you."

Olivia stepped off the elevator and glanced around. Over the years, not much in her father's office had changed. The placement of the furniture was still the same. She remembered coming here as a child after school and sitting on the sofa and watching television—but only after she had completed her homework. Duan and Terrence had been into after-school sports, so instead of letting her go home to an empty house, her father had hired a private car to pick her up from school and bring her here.

"Libby, it's good to see you. You didn't need to come in to meet with me."

Olivia couldn't help but return Cathy's warm smile. "I didn't mind. I wanted to get out of the house, anyway."

That much was true. She had tried to paint, but the only subject that had readily come to mind was Reggie, and she couldn't risk her father finding sketches of him all over the place. She slid into the chair next to Cathy's desk.

"If you wanted to see your dad you're too late. He stepped out. I think he went over to his campaign headquarters," Cathy was saying, with a concerned expression on her face. "He was on the phone earlier with his campaign staff, and he wasn't a happy camper. He suspects someone released that false information on Westmoreland yesterday. Now it says in this morning's paper that your father's campaign is turning to dirty politics."

Olivia sighed. She'd been afraid that would happen. "Well, I'm glad Dad is addressing it. Otherwise, it could backfire even more if whoever is responsible keeps it up."

"I agree."

Olivia liked Cathy. She was attractive, responsible, and Olivia knew the woman had her father's interests at heart. At least her father was beginning to notice Cathy as a woman, although he was moving way too slowly to suit Olivia. "Well, as you can see, I brought my planner," she said to Cathy. "Dad wants me to pencil in all those important dates of those campaign events. I still don't understand why he just didn't ask you to go with him."

Cathy blushed. "Your father would never do that. I'm his secretary."

Olivia rolled her eyes. "You're not just his secretary, Cathy. You're his right hand in more ways than one, and I'm sure he knows it. Frankly, I'm concerned about him and the election. Sometimes I think he wants to become a senator, and other times I'm not sure. What's your take on it?"

Cathy hesitated in responding, and Olivia knew it was because she thought that to say anything negative about Orin or the campaign might be construed as disloyalty. "I think that if it had been left up to your father, he would not have run," Cathy said hesitantly.

"Then why did he?"

"Because Senator Reed talked him into it."

Olivia shook her head, still not understanding. "My father is a grown man who can make decisions on his own. Why would he let Senator Reed talk him into doing anything? That doesn't make sense. It's not like they have a history or have been friends for a terribly long time. It's my understanding that they met playing golf just a few years ago."

Cathy shook her head. "No, their relationship goes back further than that."

Olivia blinked, surprised. She had a feeling Cathy knew a lot more than she was telling. Definitely a lot more than Olivia or her brothers knew. "So, what's the relationship?"

Cathy, Olivia noted, was nervously biting her lips. "I'm not sure it's my place to say, Libby," she said.

Olivia knew that if she didn't get the information from Cathy, then she would never get it. Deciding to go for broke, she said in a low and soft voice, "I know you love Dad, Cathy." At the woman's surprised look, Olivia lowered her voice even more. "And I'm hoping Dad realizes, and very soon, what a jewel he has in you, not only as an employee, but, more importantly, as a woman who, I know, has his back. But I'm honestly worried that something is going on that my brothers and I wouldn't agree with, and if that's the case, then we need to know what it is."

Cathy stared at her for a long moment. "Your father feels indebted to the senator."

Olivia raised a brow. "And why would he feel that way?"

Cathy didn't say anything for a long while. "Because of your mother," the older woman said.

Olivia's head began spinning. "How does my mother have anything to do with this? My brothers and I haven't heard from her in over twenty-something years. Are you saying that my father has? That he and my mother are in contact with each other?"

"No, that's not what I'm saying."

With a desperate look in her eyes, Olivia took hold of the woman's hand. "Tell me, Cathy. You need to tell me what's going on and what my mother has to do with it."

"Years ago, your mother ran off with another man, a married man," Cathy said.

Olivia nodded. She knew all that. Although she had been only three then, years later she had over-heard one of her grandparents talking about her mother in whispers. "And?"

"The man's wife had a child."

"Yes, I know that as well," Olivia said. "I also know the woman was so torn up about what hap-pened that eventually she and her child moved away."

"Yes, but what you probably don't know is that eventually, a couple of years later, that woman committed suicide. She could never get over losing her husband."

Olivia gasped. Cathy was right. She hadn't known that. "How awful."

Cathy nodded sadly in agreement. "Yes, it was. And what's even worse, when she decided to stall her car on the train tracks and just sit there waiting for the train to come, she had her child in the car with her. They were both killed."

Tears she couldn't hold back sprang into Olivia's eyes. It was bad enough that her mother's actions had broken up a family, but they had also caused a woman to end her own life and that of her child.

"I didn't want to tell you," Cathy said softly, handing Olivia a tissue.

Olivia dabbed at her eyes. "I'm glad you did. But what does all that have to do with Senator Reed?"

Now it was Cathy who reached out to hold Olivia's hand. "The woman who committed suicide was his sister, Libby, and your father feels responsible for what eventually happened to her and her little girl because of what your mother did."

The first thing Olivia did when she got home was to pull out her sketch pad and water colors, determined to go to the park. Painting always soothed her mind, and she needed it today more than ever.

She had come home soon after her conversation with Cathy; otherwise, she would have gone looking for her father just to cry in his arms. It just wasn't fair that he felt responsible for the choices his wife had made over twenty years before, choices that had ultimately led to a sad tragedy. And if Senator Reed was intentionally playing with her father's conscience, he would have to stop.

Once at the park, she found several scenes she could concentrate on and tried her hand at doing a few sketches, but her concentration wavered. A part of her wanted to call her brothers and tell them what she'd found out, but she resisted doing so. They would be in town next weekend, and she would tell them then. They would know how to handle the situation. She loved her father and if he really wanted to enter politics and become a senator, then he had her support. But if he was being railroaded into doing something out of misplaced guilt, then she definitely had a problem with that.

For the first time in years, she thought about the woman who had given birth to her. The woman had walked out of her, her father's and her brothers' lives without looking back. When Duan had gotten old enough, he had tried contacting her, to satisfy his need to know why Susan Jeffries's maternal instincts had never driven her to stay in contact with the three kids she had left behind. Instead of finding a woman who regretted what she had done, he had found a selfish individual who had been married four times and had never given birth to another child. Instead, she had been living life in the fast lane and was the mistress of a race-car driver, apparently working on hubby number five. That had been six years ago. There was no telling what number she was on now.

The more Olivia thought about her mother, the more depressed she became, and she found that even painting couldn't soothe her troubled mind. It was strange that the happiest of her days were those she'd spent with Reggie. Not just sharing a bed with him, but sharing a bit of herself like she'd never shared with a man before. They would talk in between their lovemaking. Pillow talk. She felt so good around him.

A child's laughter caught her attention, and she glanced across the pond to see a mother interacting with a child that appeared to be about three, the same age she'd been when her mother left. The woman seemed to be having fun, and the exuberance on the face of the little girl left no doubt that she, too, was having the time of her life. That's what real mothers did. They put smiles on their children's faces, not sad frowns that lasted a lifetime.

Aware that she had begun thinking of her poor excuse for a mother again, she shifted her thoughts back to Reggie. She would love to see him now, be held by him and kissed by him. It was hard to believe that they had met less than a week ago, but since then they had shared so much.

Half an hour later she was still sitting on the park bench, thinking about Reggie. They had spent most of yesterday together. Would he want to see her today? Would he meet her somewhere if she were to call, just to hold her in his arms and do nothing more?

Olivia swallowed. There was only one way to find out. She took her cell phone out of her bag and dialed his number.

"Hello. This is Reggie Westmoreland."

The sound of his sexy voice oozed all over her. "Hi. This is Olivia. I didn't want to call you, but I didn't have anyone else to call."

"Olivia, what's wrong?"

She swiped at a tear. "Nothing really. I just need to be held."

"Where are you?"

"At a park. I came here to paint and—"

"What's the name of the park?"

"Cypress Park."

"I know where it's located. I'm on my way."

"No, it's out in the open. Is there a place near here where we can meet?" she asked.

There was a pause, and then he said, "Yes, in fact, there is. My cousin Delaney and her husband, Jamal, own a town house a few blocks away. It's on Commonwealth Boulevard. Delaney's Square."

"A town house just for her?" Olivia asked.

"Jamal was the first tenant and decided to buy out the others so he, Delaney and the kids could have their privacy whenever they came to town. I have a key to check on things when they're not here. Go there now, sweetheart. I'll be waiting."

Olivia recognized Reggie's car parked in front of a massive group of elegant buildings, all townhomes, around ten of them, on a beautiful landscaped property.

She strolled up the walkway to the center building; her pulse rate increased with every step she took. When she reached the front door, she glanced around. She lifted her hand to knock on the door, but before her knuckles could make contact, the door opened and Reggie was there. He captured her hand in his and gently pulled her inside and closed the door behind her.

Olivia looked up at him, and he gently pulled her into his arms. He wrapped his arms around her waist and pressed her face to his chest.

She inhaled deeply. He smelled of man, a nice, robust scent that sent shivers down her spine. This was what she needed. To be held in his arms. Riding over here, she kept thinking about how it would feel to be in his arms again. Her life was in turmoil, and right now he was a solid force in her mixed-up world.

Suddenly, she felt herself being lifted in his arms, and she linked her arms around his neck. "Where are you taking me?" she asked when he began walking.

"Over here, to the sofa, so I can hold you the way I want to, and so you can tell me what's bothering you."

Olivia pressed her lips together, not sure she could do that without implicating her father, and that wouldn't be good. He didn't need to know that her father had felt compelled to enter the Senate race because Senator Reed, a man he felt indebted to, had encouraged him to do so, and that her father's heart might not be in it.

Reggie adjusted her in his arms when he sat down on the sofa and angled her body so that she could look up at him. "What happened, Olivia? What happened to make you call me?"

She hesitated and then decided to tell him some of what was bothering her, but not all of it. "I was at the park and saw this mother and child. The little girl was about the age I was when my mother walked out on my dad, my brothers and me. Seeing them made me realize how easy it was for my mother to walk away without looking back."

"And she's never tried contacting you?" Reggie asked, softly stroking the side of her face with the pad of his thumb.

Oliver shook her head. "No, she never has."

Reggie tightened his hold on Olivia, and she clung to his warmth. She wasn't sure how much time passed before she lifted her head to look at him. He looked at her, studied her face. "Are you okay?" he asked softly.

She nodded. "I am now. But I have to go. Dad will worry because it's getting late."

He stood with her in his arms and let her slide down his body until her feet touched the floor. For a long moment, she stood there and stared at him, realizing that he hadn't kissed her yet. He must have read her mind, because he lowered his mouth to her. She craned her neck to meet him halfway and let out a deep sigh when their lips met.

His tongue was in her mouth in a flash, moving around in a circular motion before winding around hers, taking it in total possession. She wrapped her arms around his neck and groaned out loud when he deepened the kiss. Sensations throbbed within her, and she felt a shiver pass through her body.

Moments later, she pulled back from the kiss, gasping for breath. Nobody could kiss like Reggie Westmoreland. She was totally convinced of that. They had to stand there a moment to catch their breaths. In a way, it did her heart good to know he had been just as affected by the kiss.

"Do you want me to show you around before you go?" Reggie asked her in a ragged voice, taking her hand in his.

Olivia glanced around. The place was absolutely beautiful, with its sprawling living room that was lavishly decorated in peach and cream, its bigger-than-life dining room and kitchen and its spiral staircase. Fit for a king. And from what she'd read, Sheikh Jamal Ari Yasir would one day inherit that title.

"Yes, I'd love to see the rest of it."

Reggie showed her around, and she was in total awe of the lavishly decorated bedrooms and baths, and when they toured one of the beautifully decorated guest rooms, with a huge four-poster bed, he didn't try to get her in it. Instead, he looked at her. "Saturday night will be ours. Today you just needed me to hold you," he whispered.

His words went a long way to calm her, soothed

her troubled mind and actually made her feel special, mainly because she had called and he had come. "Thank you for coming, Reggie."

He looked down at her and pulled her closer to him. "I will always come when you call, Olivia."

She met his gaze, thinking that was a strange thing to say. They didn't have a future together. At the end of two months, she would be returning to Paris.

"Come on. Let me walk you to your car," Reggie said huskily as he placed his arms around her shoulders.

Olivia regretted that her time with Reggie was about to end and appreciated that he had been there for her when she had needed him. That meant a lot.

Nine

The following week Olivia kept busy by attending several functions with her father. She had decided not to discuss her conversation with Cathy with him. Instead, she would meet with her brothers and get their take on the matter when they came to town later that week.

She had to catch her breath whenever she thought of the times she and Reggie had spent together, especially on Saturday night. On Wednesday he had called and asked her to have a midday snack with him at Chase's Place. It was then that she had met Chase's wife, Jessica, who was expecting the couple's first child. Jessica, who liked to bake, had treated her to a batch of brownies, which had been delicious. Olivia wondered what Reggie had told Chase and Jessica about their relationship, and if they knew that she was the daughter of his opponent in the Senate race.

Olivia couldn't help but note over the past few days that her father seemed excited about this weekend. He would have his three children home to attend the huge barbecue that was being planned for all the candidates on Saturday evening.

Tonight she would attend yet another political function with her father. All the candidates would be there. She and Reggie would have to pretend they barely knew each other. They had talked about it on Wednesday, and she knew he wasn't overjoyed at the thought of that, but he had promised to abide by her wishes. She wasn't crazy about them sneaking around to see each other, either, but under the circumstances, it was something they had to do.

She smiled as she continued to get dressed, thinking that sneaking around did have its benefits. It made them appreciate the time they were together, and they always found ways to put it to good use. It would be hard tonight to see him and not go over to him and claim him as hers. And a part of her felt that he was hers. Whenever they were together, he would use his mouth to stamp his brand all over her, and she would do likewise with him.

She tried not to think about the day when the campaign would finally be over and she would have to return to Paris. She was even thinking about calling the Louvre to see if she could extend her leave for a couple more weeks. She wanted to be able to be with him in the open after the election. She didn't want to think about how he and her father would feel about each other then, depending on which one of them was victorious.

She glanced at her watch. She needed to hurry, because the last thing she wanted was to make her father late to a campaign event. Besides, although she had just seen Reggie yesterday, she was eager to see him again.

Reggie clung to his patience when he glanced at the entrance to the ballroom. He had thought about Olivia most of the day and couldn't wait to see her. Last night he had begun missing her and wished he could have called her to ask her to meet him somewhere. This sneaking around was unpleasant, and his patience was wearing thin. He wasn't sure he would be able to hold out for another month. Because her brothers would be arriving in town this weekend, she'd said it wouldn't be wise for her to try to get away for a tryst at the Saxon on Saturday night, after the barbecue. The fact that Duan and Terrence Jeffries would be in town until next Wednesday meant his and Olivia's time together would basically be non-existent.

"And how are you doing this evening, West-moreland?"

Reggie turned to look at Senator Reed. The one man he really didn't care to see. "I'm fine, Senator. And yourself?" he asked, more out of politeness than a sense a caring.

"I'm doing great. I think, for you and Jeffries, it will be a close election."

Reggie wanted to say that this view was not reflected in the most recent poll, which indicated that he had a substantial lead, but he refrained from doing so. "You think so?" he said.

"Yes, but what it all will eventually boil down to is experience."

Reggie smiled.

"And the candidate I endorse," the senator added.

What the senator didn't add, Reggie quickly noted, was that he was not endorsing him. That was no surprise. The man had already endorsed Orin Jeffries and was working with Jeffries's campaign. "Sorry you think that, Senator, since I'm equally sure that I don't need or want your endorsement."

"And I'm equally sorry you feel that way, because I intend to prove you wrong. I will take great pleasure when you lose." The older man then walked away.

"What was that about?" Brent asked when he walked up moments later.

"The good senator tried convincing me of the importance of his endorsement."

Brent snorted. "Did you tell him just where he could put his endorsement?"

Reggie chuckled. "Not in so many words, but I think he got the picture."

Brent glanced to where the senator was now standing and talking to a wealthy industrialist. "There's something about that man that really irks me."

"I feel the same way," Reggie said. He was about to tilt his glass to his lips when he glanced at the ballroom entrance at the exact moment that Olivia and her father walked in. He immediately caught her gaze, and the rush of desire that sped through his body made him want to say the hell with discretion, cross the room and pull her into his arms. But he knew he couldn't do that.

Brent, who was standing beside Reggie, followed his gaze. "Do I need to caution you about being careful? You never know who might be watching you two. I don't trust Reed. Although he's backing Jeffries, I wouldn't put anything past him."

Reggie's gaze remained on Olivia's face for a minute longer, until she looked away.

Senator Albert Reed frowned as he watched the interaction between Olivia and Reggie. He had a strong feeling that something was going on between them, but he didn't have any proof. And that didn't sit well with him. He had suggested to Orin that he send for his daughter under the pretense that she could be an asset. But the truth was that he really wanted Olivia for himself.

He had discovered that women her age enjoyed the company of older men, especially if those men were willing to spend money on them. With his wife bedridden, he had needs that only a younger woman could fulfill.

When he had seen all those pictures of Olivia that Orin had on the wall in his study, he had made the decision that he wanted her as his next mistress. Getting her into his bed would be the perfect ending to his quest for revenge against the Jeffries family for what Orin's slut of a wife had done. Orin felt guilty, and as far as Senator Reed was concerned, his guilt was warranted. He should have been able to control his unfaithful wife.

He took a sip of his drink as he continued to watch Olivia and Reggie looking at each other. Umm, interesting. It was time to take action. Immediately.

"I'm sure England is just beautiful this time of the year."

Olivia nodded as Marie Patterson rattled on and on to the group of four women about her dream to one day spend a month in England. Then Olivia took a sip of her drink and glanced around the room, her gaze searching for one man in particular. When she found him, their gazes met and held.

She knew that look. If they had been alone, she would have crossed the room to him and wrapped her arms around his neck while he wrapped his around her waist. He would have brought her close to him and pressed his hard, muscular body against hers to the point where she would cradle his big, hard erection at the junction of her thighs.

"So, what about Paris, Ms. Jeffries? I understand you've been living there for a while. Is the weather there nice?"

Olivia swung her attention back to Mrs. Patterson when the woman said her name. She took a quick sip of her wine to cool off her hot insides before answering. "Yes, the weather in Paris is nice."

When the conversation shifted from her to the latest in women's fashion, Olivia's gaze went back to Reggie. He was talking to a group of men. Because the men had that distinguished Westmoreland look, she could only assume that they were relatives of his—brothers or cousins.

She was about to turn her attention back to the group of women around her when Senator Reed, who was standing across the room, caught her eye. He was staring at her. For some reason, the way he was looking at her made her feel uncomfortable, and she quickly broke eye contact with him.

* * *

Reggie had endured the party as long as he could and was glad when Brent indicated he could leave. He headed for the door, but not before finding Olivia. He smiled at her and nodded. He knew she would interpret the message.

He had been in his car for about five minutes when she called. "Where are you, sweetheart?" he immediately asked her.

"The ladies' room. I'm alone, but someone might walk in at any minute. You wanted me to call you?"

"Yes," he said hoarsely. "I want you."

The depths of his words almost made Olivia groan. She turned to make sure she was still alone in the ladies' room. "And I want you, too," she whispered into her cell phone.

There was a pause. And then he said, "Meet me. Tonight. Our place."

Olivia inhaled deeply. Meeting him later wouldn't be a problem, because her father was a sound sleeper. She knew it would be their last time together for a while. Her brothers would be arriving sometime tomorrow. She could pull something over on her dad, but fooling her brothers was a totally different matter. "Okay, I'll be there. Later."

She then clicked off her cell phone.

"Did you enjoy yourself tonight, Libby?"

Olivia glanced over at her father as they walked

up the stairs together. "Yes, I had a good time, and the food was excellent."

Orin couldn't help but chuckle. "Yes, it was good, and I was glad to see you eat for a change, instead of nibbling."

When they reached the landing, he placed a kiss on her forehead. "Good night, sweetheart. I'm feeling tired, so I'm going on to bed. What about you?"

"Umm, I may stay up a while and paint. Good night, Dad. Sleep tight."

He chuckled. "I will."

As soon as Olivia walked into her room and closed the door behind her, she began stripping out of her clothes, eager to get to the Saxon Hotel and meet Reggie. Going to her closet, she selected a dress. She felt like going braless tonight. Within minutes she was slipping her feet into a pair of sandals and grabbing her purse. Opening the door, she eased out of her room, and within seconds she was down the stairs and out of the house.

She couldn't wait until she was with Reggie.

Reggie stood when the door to the hotel room opened and Olivia walked in. Without saying anything, she tossed her purse on the sofa and then crossed the room to him. The moment she was within reach, he pulled her into his arms and swept her off her feet.

On other nights he had stamped his ownership all over her body, but tonight he wanted to claim her mouth, lips and tongue and locked all three to his. At the party she had been so close, yet so far, and he had wanted her with a force that had him quaking.

He pulled his mouth back. He was moving toward the bedroom when she began wiggling in his arms. "No. Here. Let's make love in here."

The moment he placed her on her feet, she went for his clothes, pushing the shirt off his shoulders and greedily kissing his chest. He was tempted to tell her to slow down, to assure her that they had all night, but he knew that they didn't. She would need to leave before daybreak.

Her hands went to the buckle of his pants, and he watched as she slid down the zipper before easing her hand inside to cup him. He threw his head back and released a guttural moan as sensations spiraled through him, almost bringing him to his knees. And when she began stroking him, he sucked in a deep breath.

"I want this, Reggie," she said as she firmly held his shaft.

"And I want to give it to you," he managed to say, slowly backing her up to the wall.

When they couldn't go any farther, he reached out and pulled down the straps of her dress and smiled when he saw she wasn't wearing a bra. Her breasts were bared before his eyes. He licked his lips. "Are you wearing anything at all under this dress?" he asked when his mouth went straight to her breasts.

"No."

"Good."

He lifted up the hem of her dress and planted his hand firmly on her feminine mound. "And I want this."

Taking a step back, he tugged her dress the rest of the way down, and the garment drifted to the floor. His gaze raked up and down her naked body. "Nice."

He then removed his clothes, and, taking a condom out of his wallet, he put it on. Then he reached out and lifted her by the waist. "Wrap your legs around me, Olivia. I'm about to lock us together tightly, to give you what you want and to get what I need."

As soon as her legs were settled around his waist and his shaft was pointing straight for the intended target, he tilted her hips at an angle to bury himself deep inside of her and then drove into her. She arched her back off the wall, and his body went still. Locked in. A perfect fit. Silence surrounded them, and they both refused to move.

Flames roared to life within him, and he felt himself burning out of control, but he refused to move. Instead, he held her gaze, wanting her to see what was there in his eyes. It was something he couldn't hold in any longer, but first he wanted to see if she could read it in his gaze.

Olivia stared back at Reggie. She saw desire, heat and longing. She felt him planted deep inside of her. But it was his gaze that held her immobile. In a trance. And she knew at that moment why she kept coming back, kept wanting to be with him when she knew that she shouldn't.

She loved him.

The result of that admission was felt instantly: her body shivered. In response, Reggie, she noted, never wavered in his relentless stare, and then he spoke in a deep, husky voice. "I love you."

She immediately stifled a deep sigh before reaching up and placing her arms around his neck and saying, "And I love you."

Reggie's lips curved into a smile before he leaned down and sank his mouth onto hers as his body began moving, slowly, then fast, in and out of her with powerful thrusts, stirring passion, fanning the fire and then whirling them through an abyss of breathless ecstasy. Over and over again, he made love to the woman he loved and captured her moans of pleasure in his mouth. And when she shattered in his arms and he followed her over the edge, he knew he wasn't through with her yet.

They had just begun.

He tightened his hold on her, and on weak legs,

he moved toward the bedroom. For them, time was limited tonight. Their passion was raging out of control. But moments ago they had let go and claimed love, and when they tumbled onto the bed together, he knew that tonight was just the beginning for them.

"Wake up, sweetheart. It's time to go."

Olivia lifted her eyes and gazed up at Reggie. He was standing beside the bed, fully dressed. "What time is it?" she asked sleepily, forcing herself to sit up.

"Almost four in the morning, and I got to get you home," he said.

She nodded. Although they had driven separate cars, it was the norm for him to follow behind her and see her safely inside her house. Excusing herself, she quickly went to the bathroom, and when she returned moments later, he was sitting on the edge of the bed.

He reached out his hand to her. "Come here, baby."

And she did. She went to him, and he pulled her down onto his lap and kissed her so deeply and thoroughly, she could only curl up in his warmth and enjoy. When he finally lifted his mouth from hers, he gazed down at her lips.

"You have beautiful lips," he whispered softly.

"Thank you."

His gaze then moved to her eyes. "And I meant what I said earlier tonight, Olivia. I love you."

She nodded. "And I meant what I said earlier, too. I love you." She didn't say anything else for a minute, and then she added, "Crazy, isn't it?"

"Not really. My dad met my mom, and they were married within two weeks. Same thing with my aunt and uncle. Westmorelands believe in love at first sight." He paused for a second. "This changes everything."

She lifted a brow. "What do you mean?"

"No sneaking around."

She wondered why he thought that. "No, Reggie. It changes nothing." She eased out of his arms and began getting dressed.

"Olivia?"

She turned to him. "My father is still running against you, and the election is not until the end of next month and—"

"You would want us to sneak around until then?" he asked incredulously. When she didn't answer, he said, "I want you to meet my family. I want you to attend my family reunion with me in Texas in a few weeks. I want you by my side and—"

"I have to think about my father. He would not want us to be together," she said.

"And I told you in the beginning, this doesn't involve your father. You are a consenting adult. You shouldn't need your father's permission to see me."

"It's not about his permission. It's about me being there for him, Reggie. I owe my father a lot, and I refuse to flaunt our affair in front of him," she persisted.

"And I refuse to sneak around to see you any longer. That's asking a lot of me, Olivia. I love you, and I want us to be together."

"But we are together, Reggie."

He was silent for a moment, and then he said, "Yes, behind closed doors. But I want more than that. I want to take you out to dinner. I want to be seen with you. I want to do all those things that a couple does together when they are in love."

Olivia sighed. "Then you will have to wait until after the election."

They stared at each other for the longest time. Then Reggie said quietly, "When you're ready to let nothing get in the way of our relationship, our love, let me know, Olivia."

Then he turned and walked out of the hotel room. As soon as the door closed behind him, Olivia threw herself on the bed and gave in to her tears.

Olivia slowly walked out of the Saxon Hotel, with a heavy heart. She'd told a man that she loved him, and then she'd lost him in the same day. She had stayed in the hotel room and cried her eyes out, and now she felt worse than ever.

Crossing the parking lot, she stopped walking

when she glanced ahead and saw Reggie leaning against her car. She stared at him, studied his features, not wanting to get her hopes up. Inhaling deeply, she moved one foot in front of the other and came to a stop in front of him.

They stood, staring at each other for a long moment, and then he reached out and pulled her into his arms and kissed her.

Moments later he pulled back slightly and placed his forehead against hers. "I love you, and I want you with me, out in the open, not sneaking around, Olivia. But if that's the only way I can have you right now, then that's what I'll take."

Olivia felt a huge weight being lifted off her shoulders, but she knew it was at Reggie's expense. He deserved to have a woman by his side, one that he could take to dinner, take home to meet Mom and invite to his home.

Leaning closer, she snuggled into his arms, close to his warmth and his heart. She knew that this was the man that would have her heart forever.

Ten

"You've been rather quiet, Libby. Aren't you glad to see us?"

Olivia glanced over at Duan and forced a smile. "Yes. I missed you guys."

"And we missed you," Terrence said, coming to join them at the breakfast table. "So why haven't you been your usual chipper self the past couple of days?"

She sighed, thinking there was no way she could tell her brothers what was really bothering her. But she could tell them what Cathy had shared with her. "I'm fine. I'm just in a funky mood right now. It will pass soon," she said.

Her brothers had flown in yesterday for the barbecue to be held that afternoon. It was an event she wasn't looking forward to, because she knew that Reggie would be there. It would be hard to see him and not want to be with him.

"There is something I need to talk to you two about while Dad is at campaign headquarters. It's something that Cathy told me, and it might explain why Dad decided to run for the Senate."

Duan raised a brow. "What?"

She then told her brothers everything that Cathy had shared with her. She saw Duan's jaw flex several times.

"I knew there was a reason I didn't like Senator Reed," Duan said.

"Same here," Terrence said. His eyes had taken on a dark look, and she now understood why the sportscasters had dubbed him the Holy Terror when he played professional football.

"I think we should talk to Dad to make sure he's entered politics for the right reason," Duan said. "If he did then he has our blessings. If he didn't, then I think he should reconsider everything before going any further."

Olivia nodded. "I agree."

"And what do the three of you agree on?"

Olivia, Duan and Terrence glanced up. Their father had walked into the kitchen, and he had Senator Reed with him. Olivia looked at her brothers. "It's nothing that we can't talk about later, Dad," she said quickly. She then glanced at Senator Reed, who was looking at her oddly. "Good morning, Senator."

The man had a smug look on his face when he responded. "Good morning, Olivia." He then slid his gaze to her brothers. "Duan. Terrence."

They merely nodded their greeting.

Her father studied her and her brothers and then reached into his pocket and pulled out an envelope. "Can you explain this, Olivia?" he asked, tossing several photographs on the table.

Olivia picked them up and studied them. They were photographs taken of her in Reggie's arms two nights ago in the parking lot of the Saxon Hotel. Several were of them kissing. "Who took these?" she asked, glancing at her father.

It was Senator Reed who spoke. "We have reason to believe Westmoreland himself is responsible. It seems you put more stock in the affair than he did. I was able to get these before the newspapers printed them."

Olivia glanced back at the photographs, and when Duan held out his hand for them, she handed them over to him. The room got quiet while Duan looked at the pictures before passing them on to Terrence.

"Were you having an affair with Westmoreland, Libby? Knowing he is my opponent in the Senate race?" Orin asked his daughter, as if he was insulted by such a possibility.

Refusing to lie, Olivia lifted her chin. "Yes. Reggie and I met at the firemen's ball two weeks ago. It was a masquerade party, so we didn't know each other's identity."

"But what happened once you found out?" her father asked quietly.

She sighed deeply. "Once we found out, it didn't matter. Our involvement had no bearing on your campaign," she said.

Senator Reed chuckled. "And I'm sure he convinced you of that. It's obvious he wanted to make a spectacle of you and your father. It's a good thing I stepped in when I did."

Olivia glared at the man. "You would like my father and brothers to believe the worst of Reggie, wouldn't you?" she said in a biting tone. "Well, it truly doesn't matter, because it's what I don't believe that does."

"And what don't you believe, Libby?" Duan asked, standing next to her.

She glanced up at her oldest brother. "What I don't believe, Duan, is that Reggie had anything to do with this." She turned back to her father. "And knowing that only makes me wonder who does."

At that moment the doorbell rang. "I'll get it," Terrence said, walking away, but not before gently squeezing his sister's elbow, giving her a sign that she had his support.

"So if you don't believe Westmoreland sent out these photos, Libby, then who did?" Orin asked his daughter.

"That's what I'd like to know," said a male voice behind them.

Olivia swung around. Terrence had escorted Reggie into the kitchen.

Orin frowned. "Westmoreland, what are you doing here?"

Reggie looked at Orin. "Someone thought it was important that a courier deliver these to me before eight in the morning," he said, throwing copies of the same pictures Olivia had just seen on the kitchen table. "I figured someone was trying to play me and Olivia against each other, and I wasn't having it."

Reggie then turned to Olivia. "I had nothing to do with those photos, Olivia."

"I know you didn't," she said softly.

"Well, the rest of us aren't so gullible," Senator Reed snapped.

Duan stepped forward. "Excuse me, Senator, but why are you here? What goes on in this family really doesn't concern you."

The man seemed taken aback by Duan's words. "If it wasn't for me, those pictures would have been on the front page of today's paper. I saved your father the embarrassment of this entire town knowing that his daughter is having an affair."

Terrence's smile didn't quite reach his eyes as he came to stand beside Duan. "You do mean his *grown* daughter, don't you?"

"She is having an affair with *him,*" Senator Reed said, almost at the top of his voice, pointing at Reggie.

"And what business is it of yours?" Olivia snapped.

"It is my business because I had your father bring you home for *me,*" Senator Reed snapped back. The entire room got quiet, and the senator realized what he'd said. Five pairs of eyes were staring at him. "What I meant was that I—"

"We know exactly what you meant, Al," Orin said in a disgusted voice, seeing things clearly now. "And just to set the record straight, I didn't ask my daughter to come home for you. The only reason I summoned Olivia home was to be here with me for the campaign."

Seeing he had lost his footing with Orin, Senator Reed said, "Aw, come on, Orin. You know how I spout off at the mouth sometimes. Besides, why are you getting mad at me? She is the one who is sneaking around with your opponent behind your back. She reminds you of your ex-wife, don't you think?"

Before anyone could blink, Orin struck the

senator and practically knocked him to his knees. "Get up and get out, and don't ever come back. You're no longer welcome in my home, Al," Orin said, barely holding back his rage.

The senator staggered to his feet. "Fine, and you can forget my endorsement," he said heatedly, limping toward the door.

"I don't need it," Orin shot back. "I plan to pull out of the race."

When the door slammed shut, Olivia quickly moved over to her father. "Dad, are you going to pull out because of what I did?" she asked softly.

Orin pushed a strand of hair out of her face. "No, sweetheart. Your old man realizes that he's not cut out to be a politician. Al had convinced me that running for office was what I needed to do, but it was not truly what I wanted to do. I never really had my heart in it."

He glanced down at the pictures on his kitchen table and then over at Reggie. "I hope for your sake that you care for my daughter, Westmoreland."

Reggie smiled as he came to stand beside Olivia. "I do. I'm in love with her, sir," he said.

Orin's features eased into a satisfied smile. "And the way she defended you a few moments ago, I can only assume that she's in love with you, too."

"I *am* in love with him," Olivia affirmed.

"Good." Orin then looked at his two sons. "It

seems our family will be increasing soon. What do you think?"

Duan chuckled. "He loves her. She loves him. It's all good to me."

Terrence smiled. "As long as they don't decide to marry before today's barbecue. I was looking forward to checking out the single ladies there today."

Orin rolled his eyes and shook his head. He then offered Reggie his hand. "Welcome to the family, son," he said.

The barbecue was truly special. Orin made the announcement that he was pulling out of the Senate race, and he gave his endorsement to Reggie. In the next breath, Orin announced that there would be a Jeffries-Westmoreland wedding in the very near future.

With Olivia by his side, Reggie introduced her to all the many Westmorelands in attendance.

"Just how many cousins do you have?" she asked him a short time later.

He smiled. "Quite a number. Just wait until you meet the Denver Westmorelands at the family reunion in a few weeks."

"Have you met them all?" she asked curiously.

"No, but I'm looking forward to doing so."

Olivia nodded. So was she. She and Reggie had discussed her move back to the States, and a wedding was planned for next month after the election. She was truly happy.

Reggie held her hand as they walked around the grounds, greeting everyone. She smiled, thinking she was beginning to like the idea of becoming a politician's wife.

"You know what I think?" Reggie whispered to her when they claimed a few moments to be alone.

She glanced up at him. "No, what do you think?"

He smiled. "I think we should go to the Saxon Hotel tonight and celebrate. What do you think?"

She chuckled. "I think, Reggie Westmoreland, that you are a true romantic."

He pulled her into his arms. "If I am, it's because I've got a good teacher." And then he sealed his words with a kiss.

Epilogue

The following month, in a church full of family and friends, newly elected senator Reginald Westmoreland and Olivia Marie Jeffries exchanged vows to become man and wife. Reggie thought Olivia was the most beautiful bride he had ever seen. His mother was crying. The last Atlanta-based Westmoreland was now married.

At the reception, when they made their rounds to speak with everyone, Reggie got to spend time again with his new cousins, the Westmorelands of Denver. Everyone had met and gotten acquainted at the family reunion. Talk about a good time. And it was great knowing there were more Westmorelands out there. Everyone on both sides was looking forward to spending time together, getting to know each other and having family reunions each year.

"I can't believe how the men in the Westmoreland family favor each other," Olivia said, glancing across the room at five of Reggie's cousins from Denver—Jason, Zane, Dillon and the twins, Adrian and Aidan. They were just five of the tons of cousins from Colorado, and she had liked all of them immediately, including the women her age.

Olivia had enjoyed the family reunion and getting to know Reggie's family. And they had accepted her with open arms. She felt blessed to be a part of the Westmoreland clan.

Later that night Reggie presented his wife with her wedding gift. They had flown to the Caribbean right after the wedding reception to spend a week at the Saxon Hotel that had recently been built in St. Thomas.

"This, sweetheart, is for you," Reggie said, handing her a sealed envelope. They had just enjoyed dinner in the privacy of their room.

"Thank you," Olivia said, opening up the envelope. It contained a key. And then she glanced at the card. She suddenly caught her breath and then stared over at Reggie as tears sprang into her eyes. "I don't believe it."

"Believe it, darling. You once told me what you wanted, and as your husband, I want to make it happen for you. Years ago I bought the building and when my first partner and I dissolved our business partnership, I kept the building. I think it would be perfect for your art gallery. It's in a good location."

She got out of her seat and went around the table to thank Reggie properly. He pulled her into his lap and kissed her with the passion she had gotten used to receiving from him.

"Thank you," she said through her tears. "I love you."

"And I love you, my Wonder Woman."

Reggie gathered her into his arms, and when she leaned up and caught his mouth with hers, he shivered as a profound need rushed through him. This was their wedding night. They were in a Saxon Hotel. And they were in each other's arms.

Life was wonderful.

* * * * *

Don't miss Terrence "Holy Terror" Jeffries's story, titled TEMPERATURES RISING. Coming in May from Kimani Romance.

Eight years ago Matt Shaffer had vanished out of Natalie Rothchild's life, leaving behind a one-line note tucked under a pillow that had grown cold: *I'm sorry, but this just isn't going to work.*

That was it. No explanation, no real indication of remorse. The note had been as clinical and compassionless as an eviction notice, which, in effect, it had been, Natalie thought as she navigated through the morning traffic. Matt had written the note to evict her from his life.

She'd spent the next two weeks crying, breaking down without warning as she walked down the street, or as she sat staring at a meal she couldn't bring herself to eat.

Candace, she remembered with a bittersweet pang, had tried to get her to go clubbing in order to get her to forget about Matt.

She'd turned her twin down, but she did get her act together. If Matt didn't think enough of their relationship to try to contact her, to try to make her understand why he'd changed so radically from lover to stranger, then to hell with him. He was dead to her, she resolved. And he'd remained that way.

Until twenty minutes ago.

The adrenaline in her veins kept mounting.

Natalie focused on her driving. Vegas in the daylight wasn't nearly as alluring, as magical and glitzy as it was after dark. Like an aging woman best seen in soft lighting, Vegas's imperfections were all visible in the daylight. Natalie supposed that was why people like her sister didn't like to get up until noon. They lived for the night.

Except that Candace could no longer do that.

The thought brought a fresh, sharp ache with it.

"Damn it, Candy, what a waste," Natalie murmured under her breath.

She pulled up before the Janus casino. One of the three valets currently on duty came to life and made a beeline for her vehicle.

"Welcome to the Janus," the young attendant said cheerfully as he opened her door with a flourish.

"We'll see," she replied solemnly.

As he pulled away with her car, Natalie looked

up at the casino's logo. Janus was the Roman god with two faces, one pointed toward the past, the other facing the future. It struck her as rather ironic, given what she was doing here, seeking out someone from her past in order to get answers so that the future could be settled.

The moment she entered the casino, the Vegas phenomena took hold. It was like stepping into a world where time did not matter or even make an appearance. There was only a sense of "now."

Because in Natalie's experience she'd discovered that bartenders knew the inner workings of any establishment they worked for better than anyone else, she made her way to the first bar she saw within the casino.

The bartender in attendance was a gregarious man in his early forties. He had a quick, sexy smile, which was probably one of the main reasons he'd been hired. His name tag identified him as Kevin.

Moving to her end of the bar, Kevin asked, "What'll it be, pretty lady?"

"Information." She saw a dubious look cross his brow. To counter that, she took out her badge. Granted she wasn't here in an official capacity, but Kevin didn't need to know that. "Were you on duty last night?"

Kevin began to wipe the gleaming black surface of the bar. "You mean during the gala?"

"Yes."

The smile gracing his lips was a satisfied one. Last night had obviously been profitable for him, she judged. "I caught an extra shift."

She took out Candace's photograph and carefully placed it on the bar. "Did you happen to see this woman there?"

The bartender glanced at the picture. Mild interest turned to recognition. "You mean Candace Rothchild? Yeah, she was here, loud and brassy as always. But not for long," he added, looking rather disappointed. There was always a circus when Candace was around, Natalie thought. "She and the boss had at it and then he had our head of security escort her out."

She latched on to the first part of his statement. "They argued? About what?"

He shook his head. "Couldn't tell you. Too far away for anything but body language," he confessed.

"And the head of security?" she asked.

"He got her to leave."

She leaned in over the bar. "Tell me about him."

"Don't know much," the bartender admitted. "Just that his name's Matt Shaffer. Boss flew him in from L.A., where he was head of security for Montgomery Enterprises."

There was no avoiding it, she thought darkly. She was going to have to talk to Matt. The thought left her cold. "Do you know where I can find him right now?"

Kevin glanced at his watch. "He should be in his office. On the second floor, toward the rear." He gave her the numbers of the rooms where the monitors that kept watch over the casino guests as they tried their luck against the house were located.

Taking out a twenty, she placed it on the bar. "Thanks for your help."

Kevin slipped the bill into his vest pocket. "Any time, lovely lady," he called after her. "Any time."

She debated going up the stairs, then decided on the elevator. The car that took her up to the second floor was empty. Natalie stepped out of the elevator, looked around to get her bearings and then walked toward the rear of the floor.

"Into the Valley of Death rode the six hundred," she silently recited, digging deep for a line from a poem by Tennyson. Wrapping her hand around a brass handle, she opened one of the glass doors and walked in.

The woman whose desk was closest to the door looked up. "You can't come in here. This is a restricted area."

Natalie already had her ID in her hand and held it up. "I'm looking for Matt Shaffer," she told the woman.

God, even saying his name made her mouth go dry. She was supposed to be over him, to have moved on with her life. What happened?

The woman began to answer her. "He's—"

"Right here."

The deep voice came from behind her. Natalie felt every single nerve ending go on tactical alert at the same moment that all the hairs at the back of her neck stood up. Eight years had passed, but she would have recognized his voice anywhere.

* * * * *

Why did Matt Shaffer leave heiress-turned-cop
Natalie Rothchild?
What does he know about the death of
Natalie's twin sister?
Come and meet these two reunited lovers and
learn the secrets of the Rothchild family in
THE HEIRESS'S 2-WEEK AFFAIR
by USA TODAY *bestselling author*
Marie Ferrarella.
The first book in Silhouette® Romantic
Suspense's wildly romantic new continuity,
LOVE IN 60 SECONDS!
Available April 2009.

Silhouette Desire

COMING NEXT MONTH
Available April 14, 2009

#1933 THE UNTAMED SHEIK—Tessa Radley
Man of the Month
Whisking a suspected temptress to his desert palace seems the
only way to stop her…until unexpected attraction flares and he
discovers she may not be what he thought after all.

#1934 BARGAINED INTO HER BOSS'S BED—Emilie Rose
The Hudsons of Beverly Hills
He'll do anything to get what he wants—including seduce his
assistant to keep her from quitting!

#1935 THE MORETTI SEDUCTION—Katherine Garbera
Moretti's Legacy
This charming tycoon has never heard the word *no*—until now.
Attracted to his business rival, he finds himself in a fierce battle
both in the boardroom…and the bedroom.

#1936 DAKOTA DADDY—Sara Orwig
Stetsons & CEOs
Determined to buy a ranch from his former lover and family rival,
he's shocked to discover he's a father! Now he'll stop at nothing
short of seduction to get his son.

#1937 PRETEND MISTRESS, BONA FIDE BOSS—
Yvonne Lindsay
Rogue Diamonds
His plan had been to proposition his secretary into being his
companion for the weekend. But he *didn't* plan on wanting more
than just a business relationship….

#1938 THE HEIR'S SCANDALOUS AFFAIR—
Jennifer Lewis
The Hardcastle Progeny
When the mysterious woman he spent a passionate night with
returns to tell him he may be a Hardcastle, he wonders what a
Hardcastle man should do to get her back in his bed.

SDCNMBPA0309